THE STREETS STAINED MY SOUL 2

Lock Down Publications and Ca$h
Presents

The Streets Stained My Soul 2

A Novel by *Marcellus Allen*

Lock Down Publications
P.O. Box 944
Stockbridge, Ga 30281

First Edition June 2021
Printed in the United States of America

This is a work of fiction. Names, characters, places, and incidents either are products of the author's imagination or are used fictitiously. Any similarity to actual events or locales or persons, living or dead, is entirely coincidental.

Lock Down Publications
Like our page on Facebook: Lock Down Publications @
www.facebook.com/lockdownpublications.ldp
Book interior design by: **Shawn Walker**
Edited by: **Shamika Smith**

Stay Connected with Us!

Text **LOCKDOWN** to 22828 to stay up-to-date with new releases, sneak peaks, contests and more…

Thank you!

Submission Guideline.

Submit the first three chapters of your completed manuscript to ldpsubmissions@gmail.com, subject line: Your book's title. The manuscript must be in a .doc file and sent as an attachment. Document should be in Times New Roman, double spaced and in size 12 font. Also, provide your synopsis and full contact information. If sending multiple submissions, they must each be in a separate email.

Have a story but no way to send it electronically? You can still submit to LDP/Ca$h Presents. Send in the first three chapters, written or typed, of your completed manuscript to:

LDP: Submissions Dept
P.O. Box 944
Stockbridge, Ga 30281

DO NOT send original manuscript. Must be a duplicate.

Provide your synopsis and a cover letter containing your full contact information.

Thanks for considering LDP and Ca$h Presents

Chapter 1
Naughty

I pulled up to Emanuel Hospital with a heavy heart filled to its capacity with fear that Juice wouldn't pull through. I had heard so many different stories that I didn't know what to believe anymore. some people swore he was dead from multiple shots to the head while others claimed he was in a coma. All I knew for sure was that he had been shot. I wiped away as many tears as I could then rushed inside praying for the best.

The lady at the front desk told me he was in surgery and gave me the directions to his room. The elevator was taking too long for my liking, so I put my Nikes to good use and ran up three flights of stairs. Soon as I stepped into the hallway, I could feel the tension. A few niggaz even turned their heads toward me as their hands shot to their waists outta paranoia. Once they realized who I was, they eased up and went back to guard duty. As I made my way down the hall, Juice's mother was crying on her husband's shoulder. Gunna, Mask, and Omar stood right by her looking like death itself. I knew they were gonna kill somebody as soon as they walked outta the front door. They all gave me a nod as I approached.

"Hi, Mrs. Stokes, I'm sorry to hear what happened." We hugged real deep for a full minute, but it felt like hours. I could feel the fear seeping through her pores and it gave me the chills.

"I'm happy that You're here sweetheart."

"How bad is it?" I held my breath fearing the worst.

"He's in surgery right now. The doctor said that the bullet that hit him in the back is the only one causing problems. He said that his chances of making it are really high. It's all in God's hands now baby."

I talked to her for a few more minutes until I saw Latoya making her way over. She looked like she was ready to cause a scene and that's the last thing I wanted to do. Her hating ass stayed with my name in her mouth for no reason. The bitch had a whole 'nother baby with another nigga and had the nerve to be mad at me for fuckin' with Juice. I sucked my teeth when she walked up then walked away before I lost my cool. I could feel her hating ass eyes staring a hole through my back.

"What are you doing here, lil nigga?" I walked up to my brother JoJo while he was talking to two of his homies. He looked me up and down like I was some crazy bitch or something.

"Keisha, take yo ass over there and cry or somethin'. I ain't got time to be playing with you right now," he said then waved me off.

"I'm not 'bout to play with you either, tell me what happened."

"He got shot up."

"Keep playing with me and I'ma smack you in front of yo lil friends," I threatened him.

"And the good thing for you is that you won't have to go far for the doctors to operate on you. I'ma shoot you right in the leg," he shot back.

"Can you please just tell me what happened to him?" I stomped my feet and whined. I knew I had to switch tactics in order to get the info to me.

"You're a fuckin' cry baby." He exhaled in frustration while he mugged me up and down. "He went to do a drop and got set up by the enemies. That's all you need to know right now, sis."

I couldn't stop the tears from pouring down my face as I tried to visualize what went down. All I kept seeing was him getting set up and then shot up while he laid on the ground fighting for his life. It was heartbreaking.

"Yo sis, cut that shit out. The homie gon' be coo'. All of them tears ain't gon' do shit for him, you gotta be strong."

"We gon' take care of it, don't trip."

"Since when did y'all start banging Murda Gang anyways?" I wiped my tears and asked.

He screwed his face up then looked at his homies before looking at me. "We ain't from shit except Drama Gang and you know that, blood. We got some shit going on with them and that's all you need to know."

"So now you 'bout to be involved in all his beef?"

He shrugged his shoulders. "The beef won't last long; you already know how we rockin'." He was full of arrogance.

Before I could respond to this dumb ass, the doctor came out and everybody in the waiting room got dead silent. I said a quick prayer under my breath as he made his way over to Mrs. Stokes and Latoya with an optimistic look on his face.

I made my way over like everybody else and listened to what he had to say.

"The surgery was successful. We were able to take the two bullets out of his leg, but we had to leave the one in his back. It's stuck in between his tissue and would cause permanent damage if we went in and tried to extract it," he informed us.

"But if the bullet stays in him won't it affect him through his life?" his mother asked.

"Not if it stays in place, which I expect it will."

"Can we see him now?"

"He's asleep right now, but I can allow you and another visitor to see him for five minutes."

"I'm going in with you," Latoya demanded.

"No, the hell you ain't. That's my nigga. And don't you have a man at home to attend to?" Brittney spoke up. I didn't even know she was there.

I walked up on the group just to stake my claim on some petty shit. They couldn't stand each other, but they both hated me. Them bitches knew in their hearts that I was the one Juice wanted to be with.

"I'm going to see my son by myself and that's that," Mrs. Stokes hissed after hearing us argue.

We watched her walk away with the doctor in silence. "Stupid bitches," I spat, walking over to my brother. Now he was standing with Gunna, Omar, Mask, TJ, and Flash. I could tell by the expressions on their faces that they were plotting multiple murders. I'd been around them for years and knew when shit was 'bout to hit the fan. The only thing I didn't understand was how my lil brother fit into all this chaos.

"Somebody gotta stay here and make sure the pigs don't take advantage of brody," I heard Gunna say.

"We gon' have a few lil homies stay here and post up," Mask said.

Once they realized I was in listening range, they started whispering amongst themselves and then broke the circle up. All of Juice's homies gave me a quick nod as they passed by. The tension was thick. Usually, they gave me hugs and were all smiles, even when shit was all bad. I felt like their vibes were off towards me. *Did Jamar have something to do with it?* JoJo was still talking to his homies when I walked up.

"Did Jamar have anything to do with this?" I blurted out.

He looked at me like I was crazy before he dismissed his goons. "I'ma meet y'all in the whip, let me holla at her real quick."

Soon as they left, he got all up in my face like he was my nigga or something. "Yo, why the fuck would you say some stupid shit like that? You tryna get yourself killed?"

"What? How the fuck would that get me killed? You sound hella stupid right now, boy," I shot back.

He shook his head. "If niggaz start thinking Jamar was involved, then that means they gon' start blaming you. Either he did it over you or because of you. It's gon' look like you're involved either way and that's the last thing we need, so keep that shit to yourself," he growled while gripping my arm.

"He would never think that of me."

"He never would have thought you'd go back to Jamar, but you did," He paused to read my expression which I knew gave me up. "He knows you've been fuckin' with the nigga, they all do."

How the hell he know?

"I was going to tell him."

"But you didn't and now he's shot up and for some strange reason, you're questioning if Jamar had anything to do with it."

"Did he?" I still needed to know.

"We haven't heard his name or his homies', so let's hope it stays that way. And why the fuck you ask that anyways? What happened?"

"Nothing happened."

"You're lying, Keisha, and you know it."

Before I could continue my lies, I saw a group of cops making their way over. The tension got thicker with each step they took. Everybody that had a gun started scrambling towards the exit. Gang Task Force stayed on some bullshit and didn't have any problem arresting everybody in the waiting room.

"Fuck, here come bitch ass Gang Task. We gon' finish this tomorrow," he said then disappeared down the stairs.

I sat down next to Juice's family and waited for his mother to come back out. My mind was stuck on what JoJo had just said. I couldn't figure out how Juice knew about me and Jamar. Now, I understood all those skeptical looks I had received from his homies.

"Shit," I spat under my breath.

Chapter 2
Juice

"Y'all bitch ass niggaz are in trouble now. They just gave the gravedigger his walking papers," I growled into my phone with an evil glare that reflected my heart.

I'd been in the hospital for a week with a bullet stuck in my back, mad as a muthafucka. From the moment I woke up until I went to sleep every night, I fed off the negative energy that flowed through my body. It was murderous beyond words. I went into surgery a cold-hearted killa, but now I was something different. I could feel it. I planned on taking great pride in personally digging those suckaz' graves. I spent every second visualizing their murders.

"Niggaz put a couple of holes in my body, but they couldn't finish the job. Now we gon' put holes through y'all fuck niggaz' heads. See y'all soon." I forced a smile for the camera then dropped it on the bed.

I laid there for minutes before a knock came on the door snapping me outta my zone. My hand gripped the Mac-11 under the covers just in case the opps thought they could finish me off. Even though one of my niggaz stayed posted up at all times, I still felt vulnerable in the bed.

"Who is it? And it better not be the punk-ass pigs either!" I had already told them on two different occasions to eat this dick.

"It's me, Naughty."

I sucked my teeth. "Take yo ass home to yo nigga, you fuckin' snake!" I yelled out.

I found out days before I got popped that she was back fuckin' with her baby dad. With all the shit I had going on in the streets, I didn't have the time or energy to check her 'bout it. Plus, I was hoping it wasn't true, but I knew better. The streets stayed talking.

"I'm not a snake and you know that Juice," she opened the door and replied.

Just the sight of her face made me wanna jump outta the bed and kill somethin'. Knowing that she gave my pussy away really fucked with my pride and heart. I knew I'd done her wrong multiple times, but still, you don't get ya man back like that.

"Then what do you call fuckin' another nigga behind yo nigga's back?" I spat.

She put her head down as she sat down in the chair next to the bed. "You said we weren't together anymore, Davontae. What was I supposed to do?"

"Bitch what!?" My hand shot from under the cover with the Mac. It took everything in me not to smack her with it. "Don't make me fuck you up in here. We go through that shit all the time and get right back together, so miss me with that shit! Just say you wanted to suck the nigga's dick like old times. You punk ass, faggot, bitch!

She started crying with her head down like that was gon' change what she did. I was getting madder by the second. I stared a hole through her head while she cried her scandalous heart out. That stunt used to work in the past, but my pride wouldn't let me feel any sympathy for her at all.

"I'm sorry. I'm so sorry." She finally made eye contact.

The tears kept flowing out and I could see the sincerity behind them, but that didn't matter. The damage was done.

"It is what it is. You got yo' closure, now go home to yo' nigga. Don't ever talk to me again or even act like you know me. I should have you killed, but ain't no pussy worth my life," I spat venom, causing her to cry even harder. But I didn't give a fuck. My heart was hurting, and I wanted hers to hurt even more.

"You don't mean that shit," she groaned.

A knock on the door stopped me from flashing on her. "Come on," I answered.

Gunna, TJ, Flash, and Mask walked in looking like death itself. They'd been putting work in nonstop since I got shot and it showed on their faces. They were there to pick me up so they could fill me in on the triv in the streets. I couldn't wait to bust my gun.

"What's good, gang? You ready to blow this muthafucka or you need more time?" Gunna gave me a G-hug followed by the rest of my squad.

"Nigga, I'm not staying here another muthafuckin' minute. She was just getting ready to leave right now. She came to get her closure or whatever the fuck it's called. Now, she's rockin' with niggaz that we don't, so she gets the same treatment," I responded.

Everybody looked at her like the traitor she is.

"That's a lie and you know it. Davontae. You got me highly fucked up." She jumped up and headed to the door.

"You got yaself fucked up," I shot back as she walked out.

"Man, fuck that bitch, we got bigger shit to discuss right now," Mask spoke up.

"What's the triv?" I sat up.

"We caught the sucka, Big Lex, lackin' last night and went up on the scoreboard. Did 'em real foul outside the club," Mask spoke real low.

"Yeah, I seen the shit on Facebook and already figured it was y'all. I can't wait to crush one of them suckaz, so they know shit is really real." My trigga finger was itching.

"I feel you, dawg, but you gon' be outta commission for a month or so. Just fall back and let us take care of everything," Omar said.

A knock on the door followed by the nurse walking in stopped me from telling my plans.

"Okay Mr. Stokes. Are you ready to get out of here?" she asked.

"I've been ready."

"Okay, well have a good day." She disappeared out of the room.

"You scared the lil white girl." Gunna started laughing

"I told these muthafuckaz a hundred times, I'm not letting nobody push me nowhere. I even had to argue with moms and Brittney about the shit. Here, hold this shit." I passed TJ the Mac while I grabbed the crutches and got out of the bed.

I struggled to my feet but made it on my own like any real nigga would. I slid my hoody on then stuffed the Mac inside it. I was in some pain but couldn't let it show in front of my wolves. The streets didn't give a fuck about me being in pain. They were watching and waiting to see how I responded.

"You look like you ready to ride," Flash said.

"Niggaz get shot every day, gang. Them suckaz shot me and took our dope, then went and laughed about it. On my brother's grave, I'm killin' somebody before I get off these crutches," I made a vow that they knew I took more seriously than my own life. I looked each one of them in the eyes so they could see my hate.

"Hand me my brotha's chain off the counter and let's go."

We drove around for hours three cars deep tryna catch a sucka slippin', but them pussies were in the house hiding. It was summertime and the sun was blazing, but them niggaz wanted to hide. I wanted to kill somebody. Anybody.

"Yo, these niggaz are somewhere in the house hiding with the AC on scared to death." I was madder than a muthafucka. I turned off Dark Lo and put on Finesse 2 Tymes after realizing we weren't gonna drop another casket.

"That's cause you went live and warned everybody that we were coming," Gunna responded.

I sucked my teeth. "If it was the other way around, I'd be smiling from ear to ear knowing that the suckaz were looking for a firefight. I'm tryna bang it out in public."

"But they're not. They're on some sneaky strategic shit. We gon' have to change up our tactics and really plot on these niggaz."

My phone ringing stopped me from replying. I saw that it was Jaxx calling and already knew what time it was. I talked to him once while in the hospital, letting him know the suckaz got the dope. He told me to tap in as soon as I was discharged.

"What's good?" I answered.

"We need to meet up at the spot asap." It sounded urgent.

"I'm with Gunna and can't drive by myself right now."

"It's good, bring 'em. I got a few surprises for y'all." It must have been really serious because he was real adamant about never bringing anybody to the spot.

"Aight, we on the way," I promised.

"Where we going?" Gunna asked.

"To meet the plug, head to Beaverton. I'ma call these niggaz and let 'em know we're done for the day."

Thirty minutes later, we pulled into the lot and got out. With every limp I took on them crutches I vowed to kill a different enemy. I felt like a bitch ass nigga and only a body would make me feel better.

"You don't look too bad. You good?" Jaxx opened the door with a grin on his face.

We shook hands.

"I'ma feel good when all of them pussies are sleeping in a casket. This Gunna, Gunna this 0-

Dawg's big brother, Jaxx," I introduced them.

They shook up then we went to the living room.

"So, what surprises you got for us nigga? And you ain't gotta worry 'bout the dope I lost, I'ma make up for-" My sentence was cut short when I spotted a nigga on the couch. My heart skipped a beat as my hand shot inside my hoodie. Instantly, I recognized the man on the couch smiling at me.

"You woulda been too slow for me. I coulda grabbed the heat off the table and popped all y'all, you know how I get down," Twin said then started laughing.

Twin had disappeared from the face of the earth right before the pigs caught up with O-Dawg. Once all the rat niggaz showed their true characters he was indicted on murder charges amongst all types of other shit. He went underground while the pigs blasted his face all over the news. That was over a year ago and now he was sitting on the couch in front of me. The only thing that was different about him was that he'd cut his dreads and was rockin' waves now.

"Nigga, where the hell you come from? I heard you were laying low in Cuba." I was all smiles as I made my way over to him. I was more than sparked to see a real nigga overcoming the odds. However, I knew it was only a matter of time before the pigs and rats won the battle.

He hopped up and gave me a G-hug. "I heard you let them pussy niggaz shoot you up, so I had to come home and help you out," he replied, showing Gunna the same love before we all sat down.

"They got a couple of lucky shots."

"I heard, but don't even trip off all that, I'm back now," he vowed like he wasn't a wanted man.

"You back? Nigga, as soon as you show yo face in the town, you're going to jail. It's snitch niggaz lined up around the corner just waiting to turn you in for that Crime Stopper money. But fuck it! If you wanna bust yo guns, then let's go bust them muthafuckaz," Gunna spoke up.

He was dead ass serious. The look of death was written in his eyes more than I had ever seen it. The loyalty that my nigga possessed for me couldn't be matched anywhere else in the world. Me being shot up was really fucking with my nigga's emotions. He was ready to ride with a nigga that was on *America's Most Wanted* all behind my bullet wounds. Twin looked over at Jaxx with a smirk on his face that let me know it was some shit I didn't know.

"What y'all niggaz not telling me?"

"I'm surprised you ain't put it together yet," Jaxx said.

"Put what together?"

"All the main snitches from the case are dead now." He paused then started counting off on his fingers. "Phatz the rat? Dead. Snitchin' ass Ralo? Dead. Foul ass Olay? Dead. There are no more eyewitnesses."

I nodded along in understanding now. By us exterminating those rats for O-Dawg, it also freed Twin from prosecution.

"I owe y'all niggaz." Twin shook us up again with a smirk on his face.

"So, what's next? Do you gotta turn yourself in?" I asked.

"Naw I'm good we been taking care of all that the last few weeks. The pigs have been keeping everything on the low cause they're embarrassed like a muthafucka. My lawyer has been eating them alive. I'm back to kill them Goonie niggaz with y'all," he vowed.

"That's what the fuck I'm talkin' 'bout blood!" Gunna hopped up excited like he'd just beat a case.

I was sparked for Twin, but I had my own problems to handle. At the end of the day, he wasn't from Murda Gang so what he had going on really didn't affect me. He was O-Dawgs manz and O-

Dawg was my manz, but that was where the connection ended. Yeah, we had the same enemies, but we didn't need no help. We was good.

"So, what else you got for me?" I directed my question at Jaxx.

"My brotha wanna holla at you." He pulled his phone out then called on speaker. *He could have just called me.*

"What's mobbin'?" O-Dawg's voice boomed through the room.

"We all here, lil bro," Jaxx let 'em know.

"Young Juice, you good my nigga?"

"Yea, I'm Gucci. I'm just waiting to up the score, but niggaz have been hiding," I answered. "I heard they took my dope too." He sounded disgusted.

"Don't trip on that we gon' pay for the bricks."

"I'm not worried about that at all, blood. I just wanted to make sure you were still in beast mode. I know a lot of niggaz that got shot then fell back. But this that gangsta shit y'all wanted and sometimes the enemy strikes back. So, go buy a vest then go take back what's yours, lil nigga. I'm sending my lil bro Twin to ride with y'all on my behalf. He gon' help y'all crush them niggaz, plus he still got a vendetta with them anyways."

"No disrespect, but we Gucci. We don't need no extra help. This our war now and we gon' handle our business like we're supposed to. The last thing we need is the streets thinking we can't stand on our own feet when shit gets real," I kept it raw and uncut.

The room went dead silent for a full moment, nobody spoke a word, but our body language spoke volumes. Twin glared at me like I'd just spit in his face, and Jaxx thought was too arrogant.

"That's your ego and pride talkin' right now which is understandable. You're a beast to the core and feel like you don't need help. But in every war in history, there are allies and we all need them. Shit, I needed yo help a few times, right? Ain't nobody questioning yo gangsta young Juice. Twin is a deadly weapon so why not use him? The enemy of my enemy is my friend." He lectured me.

I knew the knowledge he was spittin' was certified but my pride was fighting against it. I looked over at Gunna then took a deep breath to help clear my thoughts. I knew the graveyard was full of muthafuckaz that let pride get in the way.

"Muthafuckaz won't even know You're coming til' it's too late." I smirked at Twin.

We locked eyes and for a moment we understood where each other was coming from. I didn't see any malice in his eyes so I decided to let shit play out how it would.

"Naw they want," He reached over and shook my hand while keeping eye contact. "And neither will that bitch ass nigga Capone; I got the drop on him for you. I know where he hiding at."

"You should have told me that from the jump and saved us the time. Let's go give them bitches something to grieve about." I shot back.

My heartbeat sped up at the thought of standing over that snake nigga as I emptied the clip in his face. I couldn't wait to take his soul off the earth.

Chapter 3
Juice

"I'm 'bout to cum!" Brittney screamed out. "Do it then!

"Ahhh! Ahh!" She jerked a few times then laid on my chest. "You good or you need more daddy?"

"I'm more than good baby, you did yo thang. That shit was fire."

She laughed and slapped me on the chest. "You're silly, boy. I love you."

"Love you too, baby girl."

"I'm still mad at you for coming home after Ashley went to sleep. She really had her heart set on seeing you. I should wake her up," she started whining again.

Soon as I walked in, she started that *Diary of a Mad Black Woman* shit. She was hot that I didn't come home 'til after nine o'clock and my daughter was asleep. She didn't understand how much I had on my plate and had to do before I came home. She saw it as neglect and that was it.

"Don't start that shit again, Brittney. I told you, I got caught up. It's a lot of shit that's going on that you don't know about," I told her.

My phone went off on the dresser. I struggled to sit up and grab it. I winced a few times in agony. My back was hurting like a mutha-fucka.

We on the way, the text from Gunna said. The demons inside of me were doing jumping jacks at the thought of grave digging.

"Well tell me what's going on then," she spat.

"The less you know the better. That way the pigs can never pressure you." I sat on the edge of the bed and grabbed my crutches.

"Real bitches can't be pressured, so you can miss me with that shit. And where you think you 'bout to go?"

"I gotta go handle some business." I grabbed my hoodie and black sweats then flopped back down. *I gotta get used to this shit.*

"Some business? At midnight? Are you serious Davontae?" She hopped up and threw her hands on her hips. I shook my head in frustration while I put my sweats on. I didn't feel like hearing her mouth.

"I'll be right back; you know what time it is. I gotta handle my business and it ain't up for discussion." I put my hoodie on then grabbed the Mac to double-check the clip.

"This shit is crazy!"

"No, what's crazy is I've got muthafuckaz tryna take my life and you in here nagging about nothing! What the fuck you want me to do? Sit and play house while niggaz are plotting on me? This is life and death. I'm tryna stay alive and feed my family. This shit ain't no game so if you can't take it then let me know so I can leave cause it's only gon' get worse." I gave it to her raw so she could decide.

She sat down next to me and started crying out of nowhere. I looked at her like she was crazy while she dropped her head to her knees and poured out her soul. I shook my head at the whole situation. I rubbed her back while thinking 'bout leaving her. I knew this wasn't the life for her. She wasn't built for it. She grew up in the hood, but she wasn't hood.

"I'm sorry, baby." She sniffed and put her head in my chest.

"What's wrong with you? What's really bothering you?"

"I don't want you to die, me and your daughter need you here with us."

I lifted her face up, so we were eye to eye. "I'm not going to die, baby. I'm here forever and can't nobody do nothing about it. I'm not gon' leave y'all, baby girl."

"You just almost died, Davontae! How can you say that when you just got out of the hospital?" She slapped my chest as she cried and yelled. "You think you're invincible?"

"No, I'm just going to crush every single nigga that has a problem with me breathing. I'm not playing with these suckaz no more, baby. I'm killin' everybody, starting tonight. I just need you to ride with me. All this yelling and fighting is only stressing me out more than I already am." I wiped her tears away, kissed her forehead, and then her lips. "Just ride with yo nigga, baby girl."

She nodded her head a few times while we stared into each other's eyes. It felt like I was able to see how much she truly loved me for the first time. I also saw some anger in them too, but I couldn't figure out what she was mad at. This was the conversation that not only took us to the next level, but also changed her as well. Bullet wounds have a history of changing a muthafuckaz thought process.

"I'm always gon' ride for you, daddy, no matter what. Can you just do one thing to make me feel better, please?" she pleaded.

"What's that?" I was expecting her to ask me to check in or come home by a certain time. I damn sure wasn't 'bout to have no curfew, but I could check in with her at night.

I watched her walk naked to the closet and come back with my vest in her hands. I shook my head with a smile on my face. That was the last thing I expected from her. Plus, O-Dawg told me to put one on and not to get scared. *Picture me scared.*

"Can you wear this when you leave the house? It'll make me feel better."

"I got you baby." I pulled my hoodie off.

She helped me put it on and strap it up in the mirror. Nobody would be able to tell I had it on. The muthafucka had me feeling like superman. *I should have been wearing this bitch.*

"I need for you to do my dreads for me tomorrow and buy me a gang of hoodies."

"Okay, daddy."

My phone went off. I already knew who it was and what time it was. I kissed my bitch real passionately just in case I didn't make it back home. I told her I loved her then limped out the door into the cold night. Twin, Gunna, and Omar were standing by the stolen van waiting on me. I inhaled the cold air while I prepared my mind for what we had planned for the night. I switched from Thug love mode to killa mode by the time I exhaled. My heart was so cold, I was expecting the air to come out frozen.

"What's good, y'all ready to bust this nigga's head?" I shook everybody up.

"We got the drop on 'em right now. C'mon, let's slide shawdy," Twin said in his southern drawl. Gunna nodded his head in approval.

"Let's get it then." I struggled in the van with an evil smirk.

Twenty minutes later, we pulled up to a townhouse in the North Side and killed the engine. I stared at the house and noticed all the lights were off. I figured they were all sleep, but we were 'bout to wake a bitch nigga up.

"So, let me get this shit straight." I sat up on the edge of the seat. The plan was so crazy that I had to hear it again. "His baby mama is tired of him whooping her ass, so she wanna set him up? We just gon' walk in and smoke 'em while she walks out?" I asked.

"Yeah, that's the plan my nigga. Don't trip off the bitch, blood. She on our side." Twin sounded frustrated that he had to explain himself again.

"Bitches set niggaz up all the time gang," Omar said.

"And they snitch all the time too. O-Dawg got told on by his baby mama, so I'm surprised he set this up," I shot back.

"You wanna call him and say that to him?" Twin fired.

I had to calm down the demons inside of me before I snapped his neck. His tone had me ready to body him. "I don't give a fuck who you call, nigga. My words don't ever change. And O ain't my boss, he's yours. I'm from Murda Gang, I don't answer to nobody." I knew I had to set the record straight right then and there before it got out of hand.

We stared into each other's eyes not saying a word. It was one demon to another, seeing who was gon' flinch first. I'd be damned if it was gonna be me. It could only be one alpha male in the pack, and I wasn't giving up my role as long as blood flowed through my body.

"Y'all niggaz need to kill that shit and remember who the real enemy is." Omar tried to play peacemaker. We kept staring for another minute before he finally broke the silence.

"I'm 'bout to go catch this body. Y'all can sit here and decide if the plan is good enough. I got a score to settle with these goonie niggaz and it's time they pay up." Twin slid the door open and hopped out.

Gunna and I locked eyes for a split second. We'd been around each other for so long, he already knew what I was thinking without me having to say anything. I nodded then eased out into the night.

"Let's go up the score blood," Twin said once we were all standing by the stairs.

I nodded at him not wanting to speak a word. My anger was still boiling inside. I watched them walk inside like they owned the bitch. The nigga must have had complete trust in his baby mama for him not to make sure his own front door was locked. *Bitches ain't shit.* I made a mental note to watch mine more closely for any signs of treason. Especially Latoya because she wasn't the same bitch, I'd fallen in love with back in the day.

I crutched my way inside the dark house with my Mac in my hand, ready to crush anything that moved. I was at a disadvantage on them crutches, but my aim and the heart of a lion hidden behind a human chest tipped the odds in my favor against any foe. I'm that nigga.

"Juice c'mon," Gunna whispered and waved down the hallway.

I sped up knowing that my kill was getting closer and closer. They were all standing by a door with their heats aimed at it. My heart skipped a beat as my adrenalin went to the max. This was the shit niggaz like me existed for. I stared through Twin's pitch-black eyes and nodded. They blitzed in like S.W.A.T and I leaned against the doorframe with my heater pointed at the bed.

"What the fuck?" Capone yelled as he tried to hop up. *SMACK!*

"Shut the fuck up you know what time it is!" Gunna smacked the shit out of him with his heat.

Once he recognized the demons in his presence, his whole demeanor changed. His face transformed from goon to bitch nigga in the blink of an eye. He held his head while he looked at each one of us. When our eyes locked that's when he really turned pussy. I smiled real bright for him.

"Yo Juice, they made me do it! On my son, they said they would kill me if I didn't do it. Don't do me like this in front of my girl and son in the other room," he pleaded.

His baby mama slid out of the bed with a snakish grin on her face. "Bye bitch," she said then stood by Twin.

The look of hurt that appeared on his face was priceless. The look itself was worth me coming to his spot, on crutches. I almost laughed in his face.

"Quita, are you serious? Bitch, you set me up?" he yelled out.

She shrugged her shoulders, not giving a fuck that she'd fed her baby dad to the wolves. "Fuck all this *Love and Hip-Hop* shit. Nigga is you ready to die?" I made my way to the bed.

"C'mon Juice, don't kill me," he begged, crying like a bitch.

"Is this nigga really crying? Wipe them muthafuckin' tears away and die like a savage," Omar hissed.

I stood there shaking my head in disbelief that his hoe ass had actual tears falling down his face. I thought I'd seen it all, but never had I seen a so-called killa cry like a bitch when death was staring him in the eyes. But all that pleading and tear dropping fell on deaf ears and a frozen heart.

"I don't remember you cryin' like a bitch when you was tryna kill me, nigga. You was a real gangsta that day, huh? What happened? Go cry to the angels, nigga, 'cause ain't nothing but demons in here," I denied his hoe request. "Put him on his knees so he can die like the coward he is," I demanded.

He didn't even try to fight while they pulled him off the bed. He was butt naked and crying for his life, but when I noticed he'd pissed on the bed is when I'd had enough. Everybody played gangsta til' it was time to die or sit in a jail cell.

"Naw, you gon' stay here and watch this shit." I grabbed his baby mom by her arm and flung her back where she came from.

"Nigga don't put yo muthafuckin' hands on me like that!" she yelled with her fists balled up.

"Say another word and I'ma make yo son an orphan." I aimed the banger right between her eyes.

She jumped back then looked at Twin for help. When he didn't put his cape on like she expected, she got some act right and put her head down. I whipped my phone out then called a dead man walking on Facetime. All I could do was shake my head at the weak-ass nigga crying at my feet.

"You out the hospital huh? Oh, bitch ass nigga. What the fuck you hittin' me for? I ain't into talkin to niggaz on Facetime and shit. I don't do that fruity shit, boy!" Ace taunted me on the screen.

I screwed up my face in anger as I watched him and his homies laugh at me. All of them suckaz were on my kill list anyways so all they were doing was confirming the kills.

"I got somethin' to show yo weak ass." I aimed the phone at Capone who was still on his knees sniffing and shit. "This pussy been over here begging for his life since we got here. You sure know how to pick yo soldiers. Ain't nothing Capone about this wheenie, I'm telling you right now."

"Yo Ace, y'all come get me fam! Pay these niggaz whatever they want," he pleaded.

"Nigga stop crying and go out like a real nigga! Go for one of their guns or somethin' muthafucka cause you dying anyways." Ace kept it real.

I stared into his eyes daring him to try it. All I saw was fear.

BOOM! BOOM! BOOM!

I hit 'em in his face and chest with that hot shit silencing his cries forever. "Now he can go cry to god." I taunted.

It went silent for a few seconds until Ace broke it.

"That nigga wasn't really one of us anyways we just used him to get to you. we're glad to see you though, how them crutches holding up?" They all laughed again. "These the only niggaz that matter." He gave me a close-up of every sucka there. Each one of them threw up their set and smiled at me. Rico calling me a bitch was the only word spoken.

"All y'all niggaz are hoes!" Gunna shouted out losing his cool.

"See you soon." Ace blew a kiss then the screen went blank.

I stood still in a fit of rage feeling devils inside me thirst for another body. I couldn't wait til' I shot the smirks off their faces for laughing at my gangsta like I was some clown ass nigga out here fronting in the streets. Hearing Capone's baby mama sniffing snapped me out of my zone. She had her hands covering her mouth while crocodile tears dropped to the floor.

BOOM! BOOM!

"AHHH!" She screamed out then crumbled to the floor holding her stomach.

I looked Twin dead in his eyes to see if he had a problem with the bitch on the floor dying out. I could see that he had a lil' issue with it but not enough to trip off it. My finger was on the trigga just in case he wanted to poke his chest out.

"Twin help me!" she groaned in agony.

He stood over her shaking his head with a look of disgust. "You a snake anyways, shawdy."

BOC! BOC! BOC!

He sent three slugs through her chest then looked at me with a demonic smirk. "We done or you still wanna play who gon' put their cape on?"

I nodded then made my way out of the house.

"I ain't never saved no hoes, shawdy, just make sure you do the same thang when the time comes." Twin whispered in my ear after we got a few blocks from the crime scene.

I smirked at him while I nodded. I sat back and wondered was there some type of hidden message behind his words. *He knows something I don't?*

My mind went to both my baby mamas then to Naughty. I had love for all three of them, but could I smoke 'em if forced? I knew I could whack Naughty's dick jumping ass. She was damn near a traitor in my eyes. But Latoya and Brittney?

Chapter 4
Juice

I laid low in the spot for a few days poppin' Percocet while the heat died down. I figured it was the perfect time to give Brittney the quality time she stayed whining about. Plus, with all the dry snitchin' poppin' off on social media it was best if the world thought I was rehabbing in the house. I was sitting between my bitch's legs getting my dreads done when I'd finally gotten the call I'd been waiting on.

"I've been waiting on your call woman, tell me something I wanna hear." I got straight to the point. Brittney stopped doing my hair instantly. I felt her tense up.

"He's back in town and wanna meet up with me." Faith told me.

I sat up straighter after hearing one of my heart's coldest desires come true. Pistol Pete had decided to sneak his bitch ass back in my city like everything was peaches. He must have thought since I was shot up on crutches that shit was sweet. Pussy nigga gon' put a bag on me then leave when shit gets real. He was near the top of my kill list and I couldn't wait to snatch his soul from him.

"Bring 'em to yo house," I replied.

"He won't do it. Look, can we talk about this in person."

"I'll be around that way," I paused when a thought hit me. "And if You're tryna set me up just know we're gonna murder yo whole family, custom coffins for everybody," I hung up in her face.

"Who the hell was that?" Brittney slapped me in the head.

I didn't have time for her jealousy, my mind was on catching a body. I knew just who to call.

"What's the drama?" JoJo answered his phone like he always did.

"I need you to slide to Faith's house with me plus another spot."

"I'm ready whenever you are."

"I'm ready now, and text me her family addresses just in case she wanna play with us." I knew since he was Naughty's lil' brotha he had all the info on her. They'd been best friends since childhood.

"I got you gang, where we meeting at?"

I gave him my address then hung up with a smirk on my face. It was time to get back in the field where they needed me at.

"Who was that bitch that called your phone?" She was still pressing me.

"Brittney, you think I would talk to another bitch in yo face? She ain't nobody important, just a broad we're using for somethin'. I thought you were gon' ride with me? Why you acting all insecure and shit? That ain't never been you."

"I know daddy, I'm trippin' huh?" She leaned my head back and finished doing my hair.

"The sucka that put that bag on me just came back in town and she's gon' help me get to him," I told her just to calm her nerves down.

It took a few hours for JoJo to swoop me from the spot in his old school impala. He had tints on it, so I decided to ride in his shit. I knew the opps had my escalade at the top of their shoot on sight list.

"What's good, gang?" I shook the young nigga Ghost up. He was sitting in the backseat with an AK-47 laying on his lap. He looked like he was dying to bang that muthafucka. I could dig it.

"Ready for the drama," he said.

"Yo, how old is you?"

"Sixteen," he answered.

"My nigga a baby-faced killa with two bodies on his belt." JoJo bragged about his mans.

I nodded then noticed the Draco on his lap while he drove. I liked how them niggaz got down, but I still had to see 'em under pressure before I placed my faith in their gangsta.

It took us twenty minutes to pull up on Flash at his spot. He tossed a backpack in the trunk then leaned through the window. "Okay, I see y'all niggaz got guns and crutches, y'all on some handicap shit huh?" He cracked a joke like always.

"Shut yo ass up before I split yo shit with one of these crutches."

"And ya got ya lil' man's back here looking like he belong on a cover of a Dark Lo mixtape."

JoJo and I busted out laughing. I peeped at Ghost in the mirror. He was staring straight ahead with a scowl on his face.

"It's three whole thangs in there, right?" I changed the topic before shit got out of hand with the cappin'.

Ghost didn't seem like the type to crack jokes and his facial expression told me he didn't like none sent his way either. But Flash was the type of nigga to keep going and going no matter how you felt.

"Yeah, they're all in their gang." The smile disappeared from his face. "But I wish you would let me ride with you over there, on me." The look he gave me spoke volumes. He didn't trust them niggaz.

"It's Gucci my nigga," I gave him a look to chill out. "Just hit those addresses up if shit goes left, but I doubt it. She knows not to play with us."

He shook me up.

"Yo JoJo, since you got those birds now, you need to put ya mans on with an ounce or somethin;', he looks like he needs somethin' to be happy about."

We started laughing again as JoJo peeled out. Flash just had to get one more in before we left. Ghost still didn't find a damn thing funny though. I put on my favorite Dark Lo song 'Milwaukee' and let his dark lyrics take over the whip. It took a few seconds before Ghost was back there nodding his head and shooting niggaz with his hands. JoJo and I looked at each other to make sure the other was seeing the same shit.

"Yo who this nigga? This nigga rappin' my life like he knows me or somethin'." He was dead ass serious.

JoJo and I started crying! I couldn't breathe for a full minute. "That's Dark Lo." I barely managed to get out.

He cracked a smile. "Oh."

When we hit her street twenty minutes later the music went off and we went on high alert. Our eyes scanned every parked car in sight searching for any kind of fuckery. Faith lived in one of the good white people neighborhoods so spotting some niggaz hiding out would be hella easy.

"Spin the block again," I instructed.

After spinning the block three times and memorizing every car we felt confident nobody was lurking on the street. But I knew it could still be a house full of enemies just waiting to blow my head off as soon as I walked through the door. *Fuck it I'm going out with a bang.*

"Pull in her driveway backwards so lil' bruh can see the whole street while we're inside," I turned around to face the baby-faced killa. I wanted to look in his soul while we talked. "If anybody approach this muthafuckin' house you better let that K rip with no hesitation. I don't give a fuck if it's the mailman nigga, smash his ass. If you hear a shot from the house come in spraying that bitch. If I gotta die today, then I'm bringing some suckaz with me."

"I got you nigga, I'm with the drama." His eyes never left mine. He never flinched. He was ready to die or to kill, whichever came first.

They did their handshake then we hopped out. I grabbed my crutches and made my way to the door. I held the heat next to my leg while JoJo knocked on the door. If anybody but Faith answered the door, I was gonna push their shit back with no remorse.

"Here I come!" She yelled out.

She opened the door wearing some leggings and a small T-shirt. I stared into her eyes for any sign of deceit, anxiety, or any other muthafuckin' trait that would get her wacked on her own porch. I saw none.

"I see You're still looking bad as a muthafucka." JoJo looked her up and down like he wanted to taste her. Most niggaz did.

"Boy You're like my lil' brother," She brought him in for a hug. "I didn't know you were coming too."

I studied her facial expression for any slight change in it. I knew the last thing she would wanna do is kill her best friend's younger brother. That was the main reason I had him come. If she was plotting anything, then it would show on her face the instant her eyes locked on his. Not even the best poker player could keep a straight face under the circumstances. I gave her a nod then made my way to the couch.

"Are you okay? Do you need anything?" Suddenly, she was worried about me.

"Naw, I'm good. The only thing I need is to kill that pussy that paid other pussies to shoot at me."

"You want me to look around, gang?" JoJo interrupted. His hand was still glued to his banger and his eyes were darting around in suspicion.

"Ain't nobody here, lil 'bruh, but go ahead if that's what your heart is telling you what to do." He disappeared without a second thought. He was more than ready to make that Draco spit.

"I would never set you up, Juice." She sat down next to me, grabbing my hand. "I know we've had our ups and downs, but I fuck with you the long way. Plus, Naughty would never forgive me."

I stared into her beautiful face and wondered how many niggaz she'd tricked with her beauty. She was lying through her teeth and we both knew it. If it came down to it, she would trade my life for hers in the blink of an eye. It was all an act. Even her touching my hand all sensual and shit was an act. She knew me and my niggaz were up next and wanted to stick her gold-digging fangs in my neck while she had the chance.

"Fuck Naughty! That bitch fucks with the other side. But fuck all that, where the sucka at?" I took her hands off mine and stared through her.

It took us twenty minutes to come up with a solid plan that wouldn't backfire. I knew if we let him slip away again that he would never give us another chance. He would probably hide out in Seattle until I died or went to jail. *Pussy with money.* I saw the sparkle in her eyes as we talked, but I had no plans on letting her get a dolla out of me!

Chapter 5
Juice

We were back on our grind because money didn't wait on no man plus we still owed the plug his money. But that wasn't an issue for me and my team cause hustlin' was in our veins. We had to let our heaters cool down for a few days so we could get to the bag. Every street nigga knew you couldn't go to war if ya money wasn't right, especially if ya enemy had a bag. Them goonie suckaz hood was a goldmine so they counted money just by standing outside. But we were gonna put a stop to that shit real soon.

"I'm 'bout to slide to Latoya's spot real quick so I can see my daughter," I told Gunna after we finished his third drop-off.

After the suckaz tried to ambush me the last time we all vowed to never do any drop-offs on the solo tip. We had too much beef to be meeting up with niggaz by ourselves. I texted Latoya back letting her know I was on the way. I had been so caught up in the streets that I hadn't seen my daughter one time since I'd checked out of the hospital.

"That pussy nigga over there?" He stopped counting and stared at me. He was ready to body that clown.

Rocky was the last nigga in Portland I was worried about. The last time I bumped into him I had to put the paws on 'em and strip 'em for his lil' ass pistol. Ever since then he'd been quiet as a church mouse.

"Naw she said he ain't over there, but I wouldn't give a fuck if he was," I responded.

"We need to just kill blood and get it over with before he grows some nutz or set you up with the opps."

I was giving his words serious thought as we sat at the light. I knew his soft ass didn't have a killa bone in his body, but pussy was a muthafucka. I could see how easy it would be for him to toss the suckaz an alley-cop. A car behind us started honking, snapping us out of our thoughts. I sped through the light before Gunna jumped out and pistol-whipped a civilian.

"We gon' think about it," I replied. It wasn't a small thing to crush my baby mamas other baby dad. Bitches got real weird when it came to their niggaz. She might get on some emotional shit and run to the pigs or tell it to some snitch muthafuckaz, then we'd have to crush her too. "You feelin' them drama gang niggaz or what?" I switched topics.

"JoJo's lil bro. He's Gucci, but I don't know about his homies yet. They be cookin' them murk unit niggaz though," I reminded him.

"Til' I see 'em catch a body with my own eyes, they all suspect. Niggaz be shooting with their eyes closed, getting lucky and shit. Naw, I gotta see it."

I shook my head laughing at my brody. He was on some bullshit and we both knew it. But that's him.

When we pulled up to Latoya's spot, the first thing that I noticed was Rocky's car was missing. That probably saved his life cause Gunna was on some real kill or be killed shit since I took those shells.

"I'm coming in, gang," he said after she came out waving me in.

I wasn't about to argue with him about it, so I just opened the door and got out.

"Oh my god, let me help you." She rushed over tryna help me walk after she saw me grab the crutches. I brushed her off. "I'm good yo."

"And I don't know why this nigga letting you drive anyways." She stuck her hands on her hips and rolled her eyes like every black chick did when they copped an attitude. "Some fuckin' friend you are."

"I'm gonna go get my niece before I send you where I sent the last nigga."

"Whatever Marquis. Ain't nobody scared of you, you hella soft."

They'd been beefing for over ten years and it wasn't gon' ever stop. Ever since we were young, she felt like I put him over her, and he felt like she was tryna come in between us. He went inside to get my daughter, but I knew he really wanted to check the spot out. He already knew she'd been through the trenches with us and wouldn't violate like that.

"Is that a bulletproof vest you got on?" She asked once we made it inside and she hugged me.

"Yea I'm ready for war."

"It's that serious?" She sat down next to me, too close.

"To me it is. I got popped Latoya, what you expect? That's why I ain't been over here. I've been busy handling my business."

"I heard."

"What that mean?" I didn't like how she said that shit. "You know what?"

"Naw tell me." I grabbed her arm a little harder than I meant. "They say Capone is the one that set you up."

"And?"

"And now he and his ratchet ass baby mama are dead. Everybody saying y'all did it."

My heart skipped a beat hearing my name involved in a murder. But this was Portland where the nigga population was small and everybody knew everybody's business, especially in the streets.

"I'm on crutches," I offered an alibi.

"That's what I said." She smirked at me.

She already knew couldn't no muthafuckin' crutches determine my gangsta or tame my thirst for vengeance. That was an excuse for those soft-hearted niggaz that wanted to stay in the house while other niggaz rode for them. Naw, as long as my trigga finger was still on my hand then I was gon' use that muthafucka.

She started kissing me out of nowhere. I stuck my tongue in her mouth while she ran her hands through my dreads. We kissed and felt on each other for a few seconds then pulled away. I stared into her eyes and for the first time in a long time, I missed my bitch. We had so much history it was crazy. She was my first love. My first ride or die bitch.

"I'm always gon' love you. You're my nigga for life and whenever you call I'ma come running." she vowed.

"You had a son on me," I told myself to kill the love I was feeling for her. She knew better than that shit! I couldn't see myself ever fully forgive her for that, but I knew our bond was forever. It was her that was right by my side when I caught my first body.

"What happened baby?" Latoya used a hot rag to wipe away the blood that was dripping from a cut under my eye and nose.

I was sitting on the edge of her bed mad as a muthafucka and embarrassed. I was gripping the baby nine in my hand like my life depended on it. I knew I should have come and got it from her before I went to the house party.

"Tayvon and them niggaz jumped the shit out of me at the party. Kicked me in the head and everything!" I yelled while the tears dripped down my face.

"Sshh, don't wake my mom up. You know she gon' trip 'bout you being over here so late."

I rubbed her pregnant stomach then kissed it. She was only sixteen and was two months pregnant with my seed. I was fifteen and didn't know shit 'bout being a father.

"You right, I just came to get my heat. I'm 'bout to leave so you can get some sleep," I hopped up and called Gunna for the hundredth time. Still no answer. "Fuck," I hissed. I paced back and forth tryna come up with a plan.

"What you gon' do baby?"

"I'ma kill that nigga. He put a gun to my head while I was on the ground. I can't let that go, Latoya. I gotta be here for my child." I looked her in the eyes to see if she felt my thrill.

"I know where Tayvon lives," she said after seconds of silence.
"How the fuck you know that?" I growled.

"Shay used to fuck with him. I've been over there a few times with her."

"Where he lives?" I demanded. Now I was even madder that my bitch had been over there.

"Right off Ninth and Alberta, a block from Jack's. Go wait by my mama's car, I'ma take you. Let me go steal her keys." She kissed me then left the room.

Ten minutes later she was pointing out his mother's house. "That's the one right there." I stared at it with hate. I knew I was gon;' kill his ass, it was only a matter of time now.

"Aight good looking baby, pull off," I told her," I told her. She drove a few feet then parked the whip killing the lights. "What you doing?" I was hella confused.

"Nigga I said I was gonna bring you." She looked at me like I was crazy.

"I thought you were just talkin' 'bout showing me so me and the homies can come get 'em."

"I don't see yo homies nowhere to be found," She spread her arms wide. "If you scared, I could take you home baby dad."

"I don't fear nothing and that's on my dead brother," I vowed.

"I know baby," She ran her hand through my head feeling all the knots those bitch niggaz left on me. "He pulled a gun on you. I need you here for me and our child. I'm with you whatever you wanna do." She gave me her word.

All I saw was love and loyalty in her eyes. She'd been at a few house parties that I'd shot up but going on a mission? I didn't even have a body yet. Gunna was the only nigga on the roster that had one. I never would have thought that I would have a bitch take me on my first one. I couldn't bitch up though, so I leaned the seat back and got comfortable. It took over thirty minutes before we saw a car pull up then Tayvon stepped out. The interior light was on and I saw the other three pussies that jumped me.

My heart skipped a beat while my palms got sweaty. I got mad as a Muthafucka seeing those suckaz laughing, smiling, and shaking hands. I wanted to rush the car and pop all of them niggaz, but I knew the odds were against me. They would see me coming and they had at least one gun on them, probably more.

"Soon as they pull off, I'm jumping out," I whispered like they could hear me.

"Okay baby." She whispered back.

I slid out the whip as soon as they pulled off. I crept across the street with the heat aimed right at his back. I was just waiting on the right moment.

"Jump me now nigga," I hissed," I hissed

"What?" Tayvon spun around on the stairs to face me. His eyes almost popped outta his head when he recognized me

Boc! Boc! Boc! Boc! Boc! Shots to his stomach and chest crumbled him. I stood over him like the grim reaper himself ready to snatch a soul.

"I could have killed you." He pleaded. He put his hands up like bullets don't rip through flesh.

"You gon' die wishing you did nigga!"

Boc! Boc! Boc! Boc! Boc!

He died like a bitch nigga he was. I stared at his lifeless body for a second then jogged back to the whip.

"Never speak on this shit," I told Latoya after we peeled out. My heart was beating like crazy.

"I'll never say nothing," she vowed.

"Hi, daddy!" My daughter screamed. She broke away from Gunna and ran to me. "Hi, baby girl." I caught her in the air then sat her on my lap.

I chilled with my seed for thirty minutes answering a thousand questions but enjoyed every second on it. She wanted to rock with me for the rest of the day and spend time with her sister.

"Yo I'ma take her off yo hands for the rest of the day. I'ma take her to see Ashley for a few hours," I told Latoya.

"Music to my ears. C'mon mama let's go get you dressed." She took Lisa to her bedroom.

Gunna was busy texting on his phone. I stared at him til' he felt me staring. "Fuck you looking at lil' nigga? You ready to die?" He mugged me.

"I'll slap the shit outta you, bitch, and you know that. Anyways I'm 'bout to take Lisa to play with Ashley. I'm probably gon' post at the house til' I bring her back home."

"Aight, we gotta drop the money off at my bitch spot then I'ma slide with you. Plus, I need to see if Brittney tryna suck a real nigga's dick," he shot back.

A few minutes later, we were walking out, and my daughter kept asking me why I needed crutches. I lied about a car accident then turned the music up on her nosey ass. *I'ma kill them niggaz.* We pulled up to Gunna's girl house thirty minutes later on eighteenth and Killingsworth. I parked right in front instead of backing in the driveway like I usually did. The rain started pouring down hard out of nowhere. That was typical Portland shit and I hated it.

"Yo hurry up nigga, don't be in there tryna get ya rocks off either," I told Gunna. "Shut yo weak ass up nigga. You gon' hurry up and wait like a good ho."

"Fuck around and get left."

"Fuck around and get yo house shot up," he shot back then hopped out.

I turned off Finesse 2 Tymes' new album then turned around to face my daughter. "You ok baby girl?"

"Yup daddy. Umm, can we get some ice cream?" She begged.

"After we get yo sister we can all get some ice cream."

"Promise daddy?" She held her pinky out.

I connected our fingers then kissed hers. "I promise." *fuck taking him so long?*

I looked around to make sure the block was still clear. After I was satisfied, I pulled my phone out and got on Snapchat. For some reason, Naughty was on my mind heavy. I scrolled through her shit and saw she'd posted a new video. I hurried up and pressed play. By the time it was done I didn't know if I was sicker or madder from the clip. *Weird ass broad.*

She was showing off a building that her baby dad had just leased for her clothing store. She was all smiles and shit like she was the happiest woman on earth. All she had to do was be a little more patient and I was gon' pay for her business. But one thing the streets taught me was that the bitches followed the money. I knew that if his pussy ass was to go back to jail today that she'd be back on my dick tomorrow. But what she didn't know was that I had the ultimate plug and was getting ready to run laps around niggaz.

I stuffed the phone back in my pocket then looked towards the house to see if Gunna was coming. I saw two young niggaz walking towards me from the corner. I saw the look of murder written on their faces. My heart skipped a beat as fear shot through my veins. We locked eyes then they lifted their guns.

The shots started going off.

The bullets ripped through the metal and shattered the front window. My daughter screamed her lungs out. I jumped over the seat, unbuckled her then yanked her to the floor. "Stay down!" I yelled.

I yanked the .40 off my waist as the bullets kept penetrating the truck. I knew I had to hop out and give them niggaz what they thought they wanted before they got too close. Was no fuckin' way I was going out like a bitch nigga curled up on the floor with the heat on me. Naw, I was going out like a real brave heart, especially in front of my daughter. When the story was told it was gon' be said that I went out bustin' my tool doing my best to protect my seed. I grabbed the handle getting ready to bounce out when I heard that Draco go off.

"Murda Gang!" I heard Gunna yell.

The Draco was roaring.

Hearing the set being yelled out like that pumped me all the way up! Every ounce of fear left my body as I hopped out into the rain ready to die. I saw both dread heads backing up while returning shots with Gunna.

"Don't run now! This what y'all wanted!" I roared then let my pistol speak for me.

We provided the thunder for all the rain that was pouring from the sky. I rushed forward tryna bust one of those suckaz heads before they got away. Next thing I knew I was falling on my ass. *I'm hit.* I kept letting that muthafucka bark though! I gripped it with two hands and kept shooting like my life depended on it. Then it hit me. I fell because I needed crutches to walk, and my dumb ass tried to run. "Aghh!" I pulled myself up and leaned on the truck. I could still hear my daughter screaming. Gunna backed the suckaz all the way back down the street 'til they sped off in the car. They ain't want no parts of that Draco.

"You good?" Gunna rushed over to me.

"Yeah, I tried to run up forgetting 'bout my leg. Fuck was them niggaz?!" I yelled as we made our way inside the truck.

"I don't know but I'ma kill them niggaz blood!" He punched the glovebox.

I tried to peel out, but the truck wouldn't start. I felt myself getting ready to panic as the police sirens got closer. My daughter screaming was only making it worse. I couldn't run but even if I could, I wouldn't leave my daughter. I was fucked.

"This bitch won't start!"

"Give me yo smack nigga," He demanded. I hurried up and gave it up. "I ain't seen you and you ain't seen me." Then he bounced out and broke down the street.

I watched his chick rush inside the house then come back out within seconds. She hopped in her car then peeled out. I knew she was going to go pick him up from somewhere. She was a down bitch and my bro was a real nigga. He was willing to sacrifice himself for me if need be. There was no greater love. I called Latoya and quickly told her what happened and to come to get Lisa asap. I knew I was going to jail.

"Come up here baby," I told my daughter as I called the only nigga I knew with lawyers on retainer. "You've reached don O-Dawg."

"I need a lawyer asap!" I got straight to the point. I held my daughter close to my chest. "What happened, blood?"

I told him the short version.

"Get out the car and don't let 'em search shit. I'm 'bout to send my lawyer Ryan Scott to come to get you." "Ahh shit!" I had an epiphany.

"What!?" he asked.

"I still got my vest on." I hung up then hurried up and peeled my hoody off.

The sirens were closing in while I rushed to take that muthafucka off. My heartbeat was through the roof! I managed to hop out as the pigs turned onto the block. I stood there holding my daughter as they hopped out with their guns drawn.

"Don't move! Hands up!" They ordered.

"I'm holding my daughter! I'm not the one that was shooing! This my truck!" I yelled back.

They closed in then took Lisa from me screaming her head off. They gave her back after frisking me down. All the neighbors were outside now watching everything unfold. I prayed that none of them saw me shooting and snitched on me. Latoya pulled up and hopped out with a vengeance.

"That's my daughter and her father! I want my daughter!" She yelled at the officers that were holding her back.

"Do you know her sir?" a cop asked.

"She's my baby mama, let her take our daughter," I answered.

After a few minutes of them asking questions that I would never truthfully answer I saw the house niggaz jump out they're unmarked. I'd never had no real encounters with them suckaz, but every real street nigga in Portland knew them by sight. I kept my eyes on them as they walked around the scene taking notes and talking to other cops.

"Can I go now or what?" I asked the cop in my face. "That's up to the detectives. They'll be over here shortly."

"This shit crazy. I get my truck shot up with my daughter inside and I'm the one getting treated like a suspect.

"Black lives matter. You know that, right?" I played the innocent role.

After another ten minutes of watching them place yellow cards by all the shells and then huddle up, I got approached by the house niggaz.

"You're being detained for now. We need you to come downtown and answer some questions."

"I already told you everything I know," I shot back.

"No, you didn't, but you will." He stared me up and down. "Cuff 'em and throw 'em in our car. We'll be there shortly," He told his friends.

"He can't walk. When we brought him over here, we had to help him with each step."

"That's because he got shot a month ago and needs his crutches. I'm sure they're in the truck with the gun he was using to shoot back with. He's not going to give consent, but we'll get a warrant. He thinks he's smart, but he's well below average." They walked off like they knew every secret in the world.

I gave Latoya a nod then let the swine cuff me. I was a little shaken up that the house niggaz knew who I was. That meant the snitches were name-dropping. I was anxious to hear what they thought they knew 'bout me. I really wished I could see their faces when they realized there wasn't any guns in the truck. I didn't give a fuck 'bout that vest, not one bit! I wasn't a felon so that shit was a misdemeanor at best. *I hope Gunna got away.* I thought as I sat in the backseat watching the swines. I knew that he did though. I busted out laughing when they knocked on the door to his bitch house and ain't nobody answer. After what felt like an hour, I watched them punk muthafuckaz break in my truck!

"Y'all need a warrant for that shit! Crooked bitches!" I yelled. I was hella mad.

I watched a pig hold my vest up in the air like a trophy. He really thought he did something too. I smiled after they looked defeated when they didn't find a gun. They were hot! It was written all over their faces. The shit made my day.

Chapter 6
Juice

"I already told y'all, I ain't seen shit! I pulled over to stop my daughter from crying. I heard a bunch of shots ring out, but I was preoccupied with her safety. I don't know who they were shooting at. I just grabbed my daughter and laid down on the floor of the car," I lied to the house niggaz like I was supposed to. It was a whole lot of snitches in the streets, but I refused to be one of them. My big bruh didn't die on paperwork and I wasn't either. He would roll over in his grave. Plus, I didn't even know who those suckaz were.

"Yeah, you've been singing the same tune for the last ten minutes nigga!" Detective Freeman lost his cool and pounded the table.

I smirked at him. He didn't even sound right saying 'nigga', nor did he deserve to either.

"You know what? Fuck it," his partner, Rogers, jumped in. "We don't even care who tried to kill yo black ass, we want you now. Your name has been coming up the past few months now anyways, your time is up. We know you killed Capone and his girlfriend a few weeks back, and I'm gonna make sure you die in a jail cell," he threatened.

I shrugged my shoulders. "Never heard of him."

"You never heard of the man that set you up to get killed? I guess you don't remember getting shot up and running like the coward you are! You think You're big and bad huh? Well apparently, the streets don't respect you. I mean somebody just tried to kill yo daughter, right?" He smirked.

I was mad as a muthafucka! But I couldn't show my emotions to those pigs. I found a spot on the wall and stared at it. I was so deep in my own thoughts that I couldn't even understand what they were saying anymore.

"This interview is over; my client is done talking." A short white man glided into the room wearing a two-thousand-dollar suit.

"Big shot lawyer, huh? Either you're a bigger dope dealer than I thought, or you're protected from somebody with money," Roger spat as they stood up.

"My client's bail has been posted. We'll see you in court for the vest y'all took illegally. And when the case is dismissed just know we're filing a lawsuit," Ryan Scott threatened.

I stood up and tried to walk, forgetting that I couldn't without my crutches. "Yo Mr. Scott?"

"Yeah?" He spun around.

"I need some crutches or a wheelchair."

The next night I was back on my bullshit ready to put a sucka in a casket. I had been in the house all day tryna figure out who those niggaz were. I went on all of them Goonie niggaz social media to see if they were on there, but they weren't. All I saw was them cowards claiming I was a rat. Talking 'bout I got caught with the smoking gun and still got right out. That shit had me seeing red. I couldn't wait to make their mamas cry!

"Yo where the fuck this nigga car at?" Gunna asked as we circled the lot for a black Maserati.

I was driving an all-black Mitsubishi that I'd got from the rental spot. I was supposed to be laying low-key like O-Dawg said but fuck all that! Once faith hit my line and told me tonight was the night all that laying low shit went out the window! I hit Gunna and JoJo and told them niggaz to suit up. We sped to the red lion hotel in Jantzen beach with only murder on our minds.

"There it is right there." JoJo pointed from the backseat.

My heart sped up as I laid eyes on it. *That's yo ass nigga!* I tried to find a parking spot right next to it but there wasn't one. I wanted to be able to shoot his bitch ass from the window while the homies hopped out.

"You gon' have to park over there, gang." Gunna pointed to a spot too far away for my liking. I pulled in and. parked. I was tryna envision myself limping that far without him noticing me. It wasn't gonna happen.

"This spot ain't gon' work for me gang. We gon' have to find another spot." I complained.

"If one opens up, we gon' grab it, if not, we stuck with this one. You might gotta sit this one out blood." Gunna looked me in the eye keeping it real.

I jerked back like I'd just seen a ghost. I couldn't believe what the fuck I'd just heard. That nigga knew how I rocked!

"Nigga you crazy as crack! I'll hit that bitch ass nigga with this car before I sit back and watch. That nigga put a bag on my head," I spat.

"And he 'bout to die for it!" Gunna yelled then slapped the dashboard. "You got the keys to the city now blood, we gotta move smart. We can't afford to lose you to a cell nigga. All it takes is for one witness out here or one camera to see somebody on crutches kill somebody and that's yo ass! On top of all that, ain't no way you can move on him before he spots you. Think my nigga."

I knew he was spittin' the truth but my gangsta wasn't tryin hear it. I felt robbed. I wasn't the type of nigga to let others do my dirty work.

"Man fuck all that, a spot gon' open up before he comes out." I leaned back and waited for a spot.

Forty-five minutes later I got a text from Faith. *He's leaving now.* I sat up and looked around in desperation for a parking spot. There still wasn't one.

"He's coming out right now," I mumbled.

"I'll do 'em bad for you, gang," Gunna vowed while he slid his mask down.

"Get yo popcorn ready." I watched JoJo slide his on and double-check his Glock. I was sick.

"There he goes walking with his hand in his hoody," Gunna growled.

My anxiety shot through the roof after laying my eyes on him. I wanted to riddle his body with every single bullet in my thirty-dick. *Bitch ass nigga.*

"I got somethin' for you, big bruh," JoJo said then slid out.

I was on the edge of my seat as I watched my niggaz creep up on 'em. Pistol Pete was on point but was looking the wrong way.

When he finally looked in our direction, it was too late. He jumped back from the shock and fear, then it was murder she wrote.

"Murda Gang!"

BOC! BOC! BOC! BOOM! BOOM! BOOM! BOOM! BOC!

They lit his ass up until he fell against his car. A few more shots had him flop to the ground right on his ass. *BOOM! BOOM!*

Gunna blew his face off, and he was no longer a member of this earth. I started the car while they rushed back. I pulled out smoothly as possible when they hopped in then turned the corner securing our get away. It took blocks of driving before we heard sirens.

"His bitch ass died with a vest on and a smack in his hoodie. He wasn't built for this shit," Gunna broke the silence.

"Here, this you." JoJo dropped the dead nigga's chain on my lap.

It was his custom-made medallion. It was an iced-out Mac-10 that easily set him back forty or fifty bands. Nobody but him had it and now it was sitting in my lap. I held it up and watched the diamonds dance in the air. When I saw the dried-up blood, I cracked a smile that only the demons would understand. I dropped the chain over my neck. Now, I had two dead niggaz chains on me. One was the realist nigga to ever breathe in North-East and the other was pure pussy.

"Good lookin' lil' bruh," I told JoJo.

"You got ya little jewels now, you shining. We know who's getting money," Gunna cracked.

I found it funny how he was just preaching how we had to move smart, but he didn't have anything to say about the chain. He was actually encouraging the shit. It wouldn't have mattered what he had to say, I was rockin' that muthafucka!

"Niggaz in the town gon' think twice 'bout putting a bag on my head. We hunting the hunters and killin' the killaz. Now we gotta find out who those pussies were that shot at me with my daughter."

"On gang," Gunna growled.

"We gon' lay low and get this money while we keep doing our homework on them fake goonie niggaz. Then soon as shit dies down, we gon' crush 'em through the earth." I twirled my new chain around with a grin on my face. I couldn't wait for muthafuckaz to see me rockin' that bitch. I knew their eyes were gonna light up!

Chapter 7
Jamar

It had been a few weeks since Pistol Pete got killed and I still felt a way about it. Pete was my nigga since grade school so I felt obligated to ride for him, but the politics said I couldn't. He wasn't from my hood and got killed over a personal beef. Ray-Ray, D-roc, and Flip made it clear that we weren't putting our necks on the line over the next nigga. The shit made me sick to my stomach, but I knew they were right. He had his own homies to retaliate for him. But what really had me in my feelings was the nigga that did it. *JUICE* just saying his name made me mad!

I knew the day would eventually come when we would bump heads. It was inevitable since the day he answered Naughty phone talking that gangsta shit. The nigga had to be crazy to think he was gon' fuck on my bitch and raise my son and wasn't anything gon' happen. Only a sucka would go for some shit like that. And the lil' nigga had the heart to still be texting my bitch, like he ain't respect my crippin' or somethin'. He was playing a dangerous game that would only end in one way, him in a casket.

I had gone through her phone while she was showering to make sure she was keeping it one-hunnid. Those years in the pen taught me not to trust a soul, especially not a bitch. Everybody around me had to prove their loyalty multiple times on multiple levels. I saw hella texts starting from the day he got shot at with his daughter. She sent the first one asking if he was okay. And it went from there. Wasn't no foul shit in there but still, she shouldn't be communicating with the next nigga, period. *How the fuck he get out so fast anyways?* I didn't say shit to her about it though. I was gon' sit in the cut and see if she was loyal or not.

"Yo J-Money, you feeling this shit or what?" My lil' nigga, Pusha, asked me.

I was on the couch in the studio deep in thought off the lean. I came through to support my lil' niggaz before I got to the bag. It was at least ten teenagers standing around smoking weed with their pistols everywhere. D-roc and Ray-ray had really taken shit to the next level while I sat in those cells. When I went in, Bloods and Crips were beefing like a muthafucka. Now it was all about what click you were from. All my lil' niggaz were from both sides, but that didn't matter. We all got money and put Gas Team first. We had the most money in the town, period.

"Play that shit back again," I told 'em.

"Run the verse back cuz," he told the lil' homie, Trey, who did all the engineering.

First off, fuck the Goonies, we be droppin' g's/ we shot Lil' Mark then he told, he is not a gee/ y'all still run with that rat so y'all eating cheese/ Flocko wifed up a that right after she let my niggaz g/ Lil Shawn got smoked, y'all still ain't killed that nigga/ if it was one of mine we would of drilled that nigga/ when 0-dawg was on the streets/y'all was scared to beef/ Shawn got shot off his feet y'all ain't drop a shell in the street/ now y'all beefing wit' his flunkies/ this Mac 90 came extra chunky/ banana clip a turn a goonie to a dead monkey/and how the fuck Rico y'all main shooter?/ This the same broke nigga that went to jail for tryna be a booster/

When the verse was over everybody in the studio went crazy. Niggaz loved to hear a diss track, it didn't matter what city or hood you were in. I entertained them, but I didn't approve of 'em. I knew it was hella niggaz across the country sitting in a cell cause of a song or social media. Gang task listened to every bar then used it against you in court. But that was the culture and nothing I said was gon' change it. Long as my name stayed out of those songs then I wasn't trippin'.

"That shit was hot on the set," I said then shook him up. "But you know Juice and his niggaz ain't gon' like some of the shit you said. Especially calling 'em flunkies."

"Did I lie? Shit, I kinda shouted them out for how they did Lil Shawn. They better feel honored I even recognized them." Pusha poked his chest out.

"Shit at the end of the day those niggaz can get it too. They have been out here really feeling themselves too hard anyways. And I don't like that nigga Gunna." Glizzy jumped in.

"I'm not fuckin' wit' y'all lil' niggaz," I got up off the couch. "I just wanted to see what my money was being spent on. Y'all gon' have us beefing with the whole city before the album even gets done."

"It's only room for us at the top," Pusha said.

I nodded my head at the truth. I knew the songs they were dropping was gon' have us in some shit in due time. Soon as those Murda Gang niggaz heard the song they was gon' say some shit that was gon' have my lil' niggaz going crazy. The songs were gonna help me get my revenge for Pete. Juice was living on borrowed time and didn't even know it. I was surrounded by savages that wanted to feast on everything moving and I planned on using them to the fullest extent.

Thirty minutes later I pulled up to Irvington park and parked next to a cocaine white Benz. I grabbed my pistol off the passenger seat then stuffed it between my legs for easy access. I didn't think the nigga was on some cutthroat shit but niggaz changed every day. I watched him bounce out with a backpack that I knew had my money in it. I peeked into the Benz before he shut the door and saw that he was by himself like agreed upon.

"What the business is?" Chip asked as he hopped in.

We shook up. "Getting to this bag and staying away from all these bitch niggaz out here," I replied then grabbed the bag of kilos off the floor.

"This the same shit from last time?" Chip examined the bricks.

I looked at all the dead presidents staring at me from the bag. "This the same money from last time?" I smirked.

He smirked back. "You ain't seen me and I ain't seen you."

We shook up again. "Hit me when it's heavy," I said then we got up out of there.

I stared at the bag of money while I drove and shook my head. I couldn't believe that less than six months ago I was sitting in a cell daydreaming about shit like this. I knew I was gon' run it up when I got out but didn't expect for it to happen this fast. I thought Ray-Ray and D-roc were over-exaggerating how plugged in they were. Niggaz on the streets always fronted over the jail phone like they were really getting to a bag. But when my niggaz dropped five bricks on my lap my first day out I knew it was on like a mutha-fucka.

It was a little after six o'clock when I pulled up on the building that I'd leased for Naughty to put her store in. I copped her space on MLK and Killingsworth which was a prime location for a clothing store. The best thing about it was that it sat on the two busiest streets in Portland. But with all the shit going on in the field that could end up a deadly weakness. I shook off my pessimistic thoughts then hopped out the whip. The sun was still scorching the earth as I made my way to the door.

I kept my hand on my pole just in case some opp niggaz rode by and spotted me. I hadn't been shot at since I'd been home which was definitely an act from god. Everybody in Portland was gunning for each other, the shit was crazy. I knew how to maneuver, though, and had shit to live for.

I walked in and saw Naughty putting clothes on a rack. It was boxes and clothes everywhere. It looked like it was supposed to. A shop in its early stages that would eventually come together. I stared at her as I walked closer. She had on some leggings that had her fat ass poking out like crazy. I was thinking 'bout pulling them down and going to work. She had on a small t-shirt and some black Jordan's to go with it. Even when she was dressed down, she was a certified dime.

"What's up, baby?" I said when I got a few feet from her.

She spun around with a smile on her face that got even brighter after she saw the dozen roses I had for her. "Thank you, daddy." She grabbed the roses then wrapped her arms around my neck.

I palmed her ass while I sucked on her neck. "You're welcome, baby. You deserve it."

We tongued each other down then she stepped back sniffing the flowers all smiles. Seeing my bitch happy was the best feeling in the world to me. That was one of the main things I learned while sitting in a cell that I never paid attention to before. I was a born hustla so getting money was nothing to me. Taking an opp nigga life just came with the territory, so that wasn't anything either. When You're a real street nigga and your hearts really in it then you would eventually master everything that came with it. But while we were busy giving the streets all of our time, we neglected the women that were really down for us. Knowing how to treat them right didn't come naturally to us. The shit wasn't in our D.N.A. None of my niggaz grew up in a two-parent home, that shit was unheard of to us.

I promised myself that when I got out, I would go extra hard to treat my bitch right. As long as she acted right.

All of my niggaz thought I was stupid for still fuckin' with Naughty after she left me in jail. But she rode out a few years with me until she got tired of getting cheated on. I was mad as fuck until an OG lifer sat me down and showed me all my errors and how to correct them. Next to learning business, that was my main focus in there.

"You just tryna get some pussy tonight." She joked.

"I'ma get that regardless and you know it."

"True," she replied, still having a wide grin on her face. "You wanna see the rest of the store? I'll show you where everything is going to go."

My phone went off before I could answer her. I saw the name on the screen and knew what time it was. "What the business is?" I answered.

"I need to holla at you over at Kenton Park. Can we link up at three o'clock tomorrow?"

I didn't plan on making any more drops but tuning down almost a hundred thou wasn't in the plans either. I looked at Naughty and saw she really wanted me to see how the store was coming along. She was gon' have to wait though, the money was calling.

"Lock that in," I said then hung up. "I gotta go get this bag baby. I'll be at the house in like an hour."

"OK bae," she said then grabbed my dick. "Don't take too long."

"I'm not and come and lock the door behind me. You know I don't like you over here in the first place." She stood straight up then saluted me. "Sir, yes sir," she said in a deep voice.

"I see you got jokes, just lock the door." I kissed her then walked out.

Chapter 8
Jamar

A few days later I woke up feeling like I'd outgrown my Charger. I needed some shit to reflect my boss status. The Charger was coo' but it was more like a big ass toy. I needed to go foreign on all the hating ass niggaz. Let 'em know that a real nigga only needed to be out of a cell for a few months to pass 'em. I hit Flip on the jack and told him what I wanted to cop, and he told me to come to scoop him up. I got up, got fly then left the spot.

"What's crackin' gang?" I shook the homie up after he hopped in. "Shit, it's too early to be this muthafuckin' hot, cuz." He complained.

He was one of my day one niggaz and been complaining since we were young. In the hood, everybody called him complaining ass Flip. Which he hated.

"Shut yo cryin' ass up nigga. You the one came out in the heat rockin' a hoodie."

"Cause of this, lil' nigga." He yanked out a Draco then laid it on his lap.

"Where we going?"

"To the slob niggaz Breeze car lot, it's downtown right off burnside. I already let 'em know we're on the way."

I peeled out headed downtown. We were coo' with the Hit squad niggaz so I was confused on why he felt the need to bring a Draco with the monkey nuts on it."

"We still on good terms with these niggaz right?" I asked.

"Yea, why you ask that?" He had a confused look on his face.

"Cause you brought the Draco with you and you called him a slob."

"Any blood that's not on our side is a slob, period. And the homies feel that any Crip that ain't gang is a crab. That's just the way it is. And this pretty muthafucka is for any nigga that thinks shit is sweet. Ever since Pusha dropped that diss track niggaz been talkin' reckless on the net. I'm letting this muthafucka off wherever I catch a nigga at."

"Yea, I saw all that clown shit."

From the moment the song dropped it was pure internet banging at its finest. From everything to videos, to gun emoji's, to disrespectful pictures, niggaz were going wild. I already knew somebody was gon' get shot before it was all said and done.

"All type of muthafuckaz got somethin' to say. Most of them bitch niggaz weren't even from Goonies."

"That's cause he said niggaz names that ain't from over there," I replied.

"The damage is done cuz." He spat back then gripped the Draco.

He'd always been gun-happy since day one, so his temper tantrum wasn't nothing new to me. I knew he meant every word that came out of his mouth. He was gon' pop somebody for any reason he could come up with. I shook my head then turned up *WAR* by Pop smoke.

Twenty minutes later we pulled into the car lot downtown then hopped out. It was luxury cars parked everywhere. I knew I was leaving in something foreign. I brushed the hood of a Lamborghini and thought about copping that bitch. *Too flashy* I shook off the thrill that would definitely get the feds on me.

"This nigga really getting his money, huh? Now I see how all his niggaz be coppin' those whips," I said to Flip.

"Yea, he doing his thang." He sounded unimpressed.

We walked inside and a pretty white chick immediately came over to service us. Once I realized we were the only ones inside I started to relax a bit. The way Flip was talking in the car made me leave the bag of money in it and had my gun glued to my waist.

"We're here to holla at the owner." He cut off her sales pitch.

"Oh ok, he's expecting you. Let me go get him for you." She replied then disappeared in the back.

I walked over to a black Maserati and fell in love with it. I used to daydream 'bout pulling up in one when I was in that cold cell. It was a couple of whips on my list and the 'Rati was definitely at the top. I peeped at the price tag then nodded at it. I had that in the duffle bag.

"What's good with y'all niggaz.?" Breeze walked over with his arms in the air like he was happy to see us.

He had on some linen pants and a Burberry button-up with matching loafers. At that moment I knew everything was on the up and up. He was dressed to get a bag, not rob a nigga or whatever else was running through Flip's mind. I didn't even see a bulge on his waist. *He the one that's slippin'*

"What's good? I'm tryna cop somethin' foreign on all these hating ass niggaz out here," I told him as we shook hands.

"You ready to step it up huh?" He replied then shook hands with Flip. "It looks like you feeling this bitch right here?"

"Definitely, but I'm feeling that hoe over there even more." I pointed at the coke white 600 Benz.

I walked over to her and rubbed her down. If it was one car, I daydreamed about the most the S600 had to be the one. The Maserati was no longer on my mind as I opened the door then sat behind the wheel.

"We just got this one." Breeze told me.

"And you just sold it, too."

"I'ma need a buck seventy-five for it. I'ma hook the paperwork up for you and all that good shit, but I'ma need all cash.

I was picturing all the bitches throwing their panties at a nigga. Niggaz was already hating on my come-up, I couldn't wait to see their faces now.

"I got yo bread in the car my nigga. Let's get this shit done," I told Flip 20 minutes later.

"Meet me at my spot," I told Flip, then peeled out the lot.

I couldn't feel the ground as I pushed the big body down the street. It felt like a nigga was floating on thin air. I was riding like a real boss was supposed to. I took my shirt off then rolled the windows down. I let the sun shine on all my diamonds while I floated through the North-East. I pulled my phone out then let Snapchat see how I was living. I wasn't with that talking on the net shit, so I let pop smoke do it for me.

I tossed the phone then gripped the smack just in case I bumped into an opp nigga. I knew it was hella niggaz that would love to take my life just because they wanted what I had. Niggaz in Portland was grimy like that. But any nigga that wanted my life or anything else from me was gon' have to be willing to sacrifice their soul. A nigga wasn't getting shit from me except a clip full of hot shit!

"Gas team! Tell y'all baby daddies to step their shit up." I yelled at a group of hoodrats that were walking inside a gas station. I leaned out the window so they could store the image in their memory. I was the muthafuckin' epitome of fly crippin'

"Fuck my baby daddy!" one yelled.

"I don't got one! But you can mine!" another yelled.

"Gas team J-money! Google me." I threw the setup since they had their cameras out.

I bent the corner and disappeared on them bitches. I knew they would be in my inbox before the night was over. I rolled slowly down the streets so everybody could see me until I made it to my spot. When I pulled up Flip was standing in the driveway with his arms out. I knew he had an attitude before I even hopped out.

"Yo cuz, take some flicks of me sitting on the big body. I'm 'bout to have Snapchat going crazy, on me." I tried to hand him my phone.

He pushed my hand away. "Cuz who the fuck you think you are hoppin' out with yo shirt off and shit? Lil Wayne? C'mon, we gotta slide. The opps caught Glizzy lackin' and got 'em." He jumped in the whip looking ready to body somebody.

Chapter 9
Jamar

My heart skipped a beat. *They killed my lil nigga.* I was just with 'em the other day and now the enemy had got to him. *Damn Glizzy.* I gritted my teeth as I hopped in with murder on my mind.

"Where they kill 'em at?"

"They ain't kill nobody," He screwed his face up. He whipped his phone out then clicked on a video. "They caught 'em at the mall then stripped 'em for his jewels."

I stared at the screen in disbelief. I couldn't believe he'd let those suckaz catch 'em like that. I watched a group of ten niggaz approach Glizzy real hostile. He walked backwards then tried to run. He must didn't have a pistol on him and figured it was a no-win situation.

But he didn't get far, especially with bags in his hands. They tripped 'em to the ground and it was over from there. They hit my nigga with a hundred hooks while they stomped him out. Niggaz were throwing up goonies while talking shit at the same time. I recognized most of them and burned the rest of 'em in my memory. After they ran through his pockets and took his watch they yelled 'fuck Gas Team'. And 'tell Pusha he next!' I shook my head mad as a muthafucka.

"He went out like a bitch!" Flip screamed then punched the glovebox.

"They were deep, and we know they had some thangs on 'em," I tried to defend his actions.

"Nigga what? Ain't nobody 'bout to body nobody in the mall and you know it. His bitch ass knew they wasn't 'bout to shoot him in there."

My phone went off. I saw it was ray-ray and answered it on speaker. "What it is?" I answered.

"I see you copped the big body."

"Yea I had to step it up."

"You hear 'bout the shit with Glizzy?"

I looked at Flip. "Yea, Flip just showed me the video. He mad as a muthafucka too, especially at Glizzy."

"y'all come fuck with me at my spot." He hung up before I could reply. I already knew what he wanted to holla about. It was time to push the button.

"Man cuz, why the fuck that nigga want us to come way out to Salem? That shit like forty-five minutes away, shit. He could have said the shit over the phone. Niggaz start moving a few birds then think they Big Meech and shit," he vented.

"Naw, it's just smart to not talk on the jack and you know that. Just sit back and enjoy the ride nigga."

"Whatever nigga."

I turned on Lil Durk and let the music drown out his complaining. The situation with Glizzy mixed with flips pessimistic ass was really fuckin' with my vibe. A nigga wasn't posed to be stressed out sitting in a 600. I inhaled the smell of a new foreign and relaxed my nerves. Whatever was gon' happen was gon' happen, period.

By the time we pulled up to Ray-Ray's mini mansion, the heat felt like it had risen at least thirty degrees. This was the type of heat that got niggaz killed in every ghetto in America.

"What's brackin' wit' y'all?" He shook us up then let us in.

"Nigga, why the fuck you live way out here?" Flip asked.

"Cause niggaz can't get to me way out here. Plus, I don't want my kids or baby mama to be targeted in Portland," he replied while leading us into the living room.

I thought hard about what he said while I looked around at all the expensive decorations that I knew his baby mama spent a fortune on. *this nigga really living.* I knew I had to step my hustle up if I wanted to level up.

"I gotta get one of these," I spread my arms after I sat down. "This shit makes my house look like an apartment."

"You on the way nigga, we gon' get you here." You already running laps on niggaz out here. Whenever you ready to up the order just let me know. I'ma hit you off with whatever you can handle, on me"

"Off top, say less." I shook my nigga up again ready to get a bigger bag.

Just being in the presence of money made me wanna get up and cook a brick. I'd been knowing the nigga my whole life, so I knew how far he'd come. If he could do it then I knew it was nothing for me to do it. I was hungry with a family to feed.

"You holla at D-roc 'bout Glizzy?" Flip got straight to the point.

"Yea he wants y'all to handle it before he gets back from Miami. He said it's y'all job to handle all the petty shit while we keep the plug happy."

"Oh, we gon' handle it, believe that. I wanna know how y'all feel 'bout the lil' nigga?"

Ray-ray lifted his arms up. "Either he put that work in or he dead to us. He always been a stand-up nigga, I doubt it'll be a problem."

"We'll figure it out," I added.

"This gon' be yo chance to show the lil' niggaz how you get down. Earn their respect fo'real. They fuck with you off the strength of yo name and how hard you be getting to a bag. But they don't really know how you get down with that thang. It's time to show 'em."

I nodded my head. "We gon' figure it out." I knew he was spittin' the truth.

It had been a long time since I'd busted my gun in Portland. A whole lot of niggaz either didn't know my get down or forgotten it. But that was expected. The streets have a short-term memory. Anytime yo gun went warm that's when niggaz started to test you. We chopped it up with ray-ray for another ten minutes then left with a war on our minds. It was do-or-die time, and I had no plans on dying anytime soon.

"Bitch ass niggaz with money." Flip vented as soon as we pulled off.

"That's how you feel cuz?" I asked. *This nigga trippin'.*

He sucked his teeth. "Ain't neither one of those niggas bust their guns in over a year. They got a hundred choppaz with dust bunnies in the barrels. Money turn niggaz soft on the set!" He really felt some type of way.

"You right, sometimes it does. But it also makes you smarter too. When you level up, you gotta move differently."

"Cuz what the fuck that got to do with niggaz acting like hoes?" he spat.

I shook my head. "When You're rich sometimes you gotta make moves that look soft to a bunch of broke niggaz." I tried to explain.

"You learn that in jail too? That's in the forty-eight laws of power? They got a street edition?" He was shooting shots now. I tuned the music down. Now I felt some type of way.

"Naw muthafucka! I learnt it from being in the streets my whole life. The nigga with the bag ain't supposed to put himself in jeopardy. He supposed to feed the wolves cuz."

"So, you agree with them niggaz playing house?" He had a look of disappointment on his face.

"Hell yea, nigga," I replied with no hesitation. "If I was in Miami with the plug, these lil' weak ass niggaz wouldn't even cross my mind. Niggaz droppin' songs, talkin' on the net, and making videos. Ain't none of that shit gangsta to me. It's either niggaz gon' die or not," I vented.

I turned Lil Durk all the way up. I didn't even wanna hear what he had to say. It was pointless cause he was only able to think one way. He was a shooter that got money and that would never change. I wanted to be the nigga with the bag that would shoot if necessary.

Chapter 10
Jamar

The next night we were all packed inside the studio having a gangsta meeting. There wasn't a smile in the room. The tension was so thick it could be felt throughout the whole room. I knew somebody was gonna die tonight, it was inevitable. Every time I looked at Glizzy's face it made me wanna kill somebody. He had a black eye, swollen lips, and stitches in his face. They fucked my nigga up.

"Cuz I'm tryna figure out why you thought it was coo' to run like a bitch. This whole time you've been talkin' 'bout revenge and shit but I ain't heard shit about that." Flip interrupted Glizzy.

I knew he was gon' say something. I shook my head already knowing where shit was about to go. The room got dead silent instantly. Everybody looked from Flip to Glizzy in anticipation.

"Nigga don't mention my name and bitch in the same sentence," Glizzy growled. The challenge was issued.

"I already said what I said, nigga, and I can't take it back," Flip spat. "So, what's next?"

A deadly scowl appeared on Glizzy's face then he popped up off the couch. I noticed his hand was a little too close to his waist. "So, what the fuck you tryna say? I'ma bitch or somethin'?"

Flip stood up real slow like he ain't have a care in the world. His body language was nonchalant, but his eyes were murderous.

"I said exactly what I meant. When you tried to run, that was a bitch move and I'm highly disappointed. You made yourself and the whole team look weak. But if you don't move yo hand from yo waist then one of us gon' die real soon. Your call."

"Y'all niggaz chill out blood." T-Rex got in between them.

They stared each other down but I noticed Glizzy relocate his hand. I didn't intervene because I knew men had to be men. The last thing a crew needed during wartime was an elephant in the room. All tension had to be eradicated. If niggaz had to throw hands, then so be it. If guns get pulled, so be it.

"That's how y'all niggaz really feel? Niggaz think I went out like a bitch?" Glizzy held his arms out challenging the whole room. He made eye contact with every single person.

Most of the room nodded in agreement with Flip. Glizzy looked shocked that niggaz felt that way about him. A mask of anger replaced the shock within seconds then the fire came to his eyes.

"Aight, I'ma show y'all niggaz wassup with me, on the dead homies. I'ma be the first one to smoke one of those fuck niggaz. He growled then sat down. He had smoke coming out of his ears.

"As you should," Flip said then shook him up, killing any tension that may have still been there. Then he stood in

the middle of the room.

"We can never let the enemy embarrass us, even if that means death. An attack on one of us is an attack on all of us. We gotta go put the fear back in those niggaz soft ass chests. We should have been wiped those pussies out, but we have been playing. Go get y'all manz and do it soon. It better be some slow singing and flower bringing

within the week." He commanded then sat down.

I sat back and listened to everybody vow revenge and toss out spots they were gonna hit up. I didn't feel the need to speak it was enough of that going on. My mind was stuck on the fact that we were going to war. I hadn't been out of jail for six months and it was already time to suit up. I stared at all the homies' faces and all I saw was smile and grins. They thought the shit was a joke when it wasn't. They were used to everybody bowing down. Our movement was so big and powerful that most of Portland let us step all over them. I knew most of my lil' niggaz hadn't been in a real war. I looked around and wondered who was gon' be the first one to die out of the clan. I knew that even the side that won always took a few losses. I was gon' do everything in my power to prevent that from happening though. It was only one way to do that. Apply pressure.

"Glizzy, you and Pusha come rock with me," I stood up and stretched, tired of all the talking. "We ''bout to go start this shit off right."

"Let's go get it then." Pusha hopped up ready to put the work in.

Glizzy nodded then walked out without uttering a word. He was really in his feelings.

"This our time to shine," Flip gave me a g-hug. "We ''bout to show niggaz who really run the town."

I nodded. "Say less." I made my way out of the room.

It wasn't as cold as I'd expected it to be. It was almost midnight but the heat from earlier could still be felt. "C'mon we taking the Benz. Ain't nobody gon' expect for nobody to be head hunting in that muthafucka. We

gon' have the element of surprise on our side," I told the homies as we hopped in.

They both got in the back with matching scowls on their faces. I texted Naughty letting her know I wouldn't be home til' the morning.

"Where y'all wanna go first?" I asked.

"slide by Kenton park, a few of them niggaz live over there. I heard they be posted up over there on the regular." Glizzy spoke up.

I eased out into the night. There wasn't any traffic out on the streets, so we turned a twenty-minute drive into ten. "Y'all keep ya eyes open." I turned the music down then told my young goons. I killed the lights as I maneuvered around the park.

"There go somebody right there cuz!" Glizzy got excited.

I looked in the direction he was pointing at. It was a young nigga and a bitch walking all cuddled up and shit. I pulled up right next to them. "Let's check this nigga temperature," I said.

"He bet not have one if he wanna live," Pusha replied.

We slid out with our heats aimed right at his dome, daring him to move. His chick gasped then covered her mouth with her hands.

"Sup cuz, what hood you from?" I kept the heat on 'em as we walked closer.

"I don't bang fam." Fear shot through his body as his hands shot in the air in surrender mode.

"Stop lying bitch ass nigga, rep yo hood." Glizzy got up in his face then started patting him down. He wanted to take somebody's life badly.

"You know cuz?" I asked Pusha. It was impossible for any nigga to deny his affiliation nowadays with social media.

"Naw." He shook his head real slow while he stared dude up and down for the slightest recognition. "What's yo name lil' nigga?"

"Leroy." He was shaking like a stripper.

The name didn't ring a bell. The more I stared into his eyes the more I felt he wasn't no street nigga. But that didn't mean he wasn't the brother of one of our enemies. And if he was then he was gon' die for his family's sins, period.

"So, you telling me that you live over here, but you don't bang? You don't fuck with the goonies either, huh? If you lie to me, I'ma crush you right now," I threatened.

"I don't even live over here I swear to god. I came over here to come to my girl's house, that's it," he pleaded his case.

I knew he was telling the truth. I turned my attention to his bitch.

"Where them niggaz at?" I growled. "If you say you don't know, I'ma spank you and yo boyfriend right here, right now. That's on my son." I was done playing games.

"They be around the corner standing in front of the house on the corner. That's all I know, I swear." She pointed us in the direction. She knew I wasn't playing.

"Yo, if you don't wanna die young then I suggest you stop coming over here. This bitch ''bout to turn into Iraq." I warned then hopped back in the whip.

I eased the Benz around the corner then crept down the street searching for the enemy. "We should have slumped both of them," Glizzy vented.

"Look cuz!" I raised my voice in frustration. I was tired of the nigga complaining and wanting to do dumb ass shit. "Innocent bodies don't count, that shit is for cowards. I'm not gon' be the nigga with the life sentence for killin' a nobody, fuck that. We gon' be patient til' we catch one of these pussies slippin' then blow they head off, period. You've been in yo feelings ever since the meeting. Emotions either get you killed or in a cell. Kill yo emotions if you wanna survive."

He nodded then leaned back in silence. It was no need to speak. He knew I was spittin' the truth. Soon as I started driving again, I spotted a nigga walking up the stairs to a house that sat on the corner. *There it goes!*

"There go one of those suckaz right there cuz," I whispered.

They both jumped out of their seats to get a better look. I kept driving slow right by the house. It was about five niggaz standing on the porch looking like they were with the shit. All eyes were on the Benz as we crept by. I could feel the tension aimed at us. I was hoping they couldn't feel the tension we had reserved for them. My heart was pounding through my chest.

"Be cool," I demanded. Glizzy looked ready to bounce out. I saw one of the suckaz ease his hand to his waist.

"That's man-man right there," Pusha growled.

"Chill."

We made it past them without having to shoot for our lives. I bent the corner then bent another before I killed the engine. We found what we were looking for and now it was time to show niggaz that we weren't to be fucked with.

"Y'all know the drill. We gon' walk up on them pussies, shoot 'em in the face then hop back in. Keep bustin' that bitch til' you run out or all of them suckaz are dead. We gotta make this shit count cuz." I lectured my hittaz.

"I'm ready right now," Pusha said.

"We gon' wait five minutes, give 'em time to get settled in. Y'all turn them phones off and leave 'em in the car."

We waited ten minutes just to be safe before we bounced out into the night with our burners hanging by our legs. I glanced at both of them to make sure I saw no signs of pussy. I was satisfied with what I saw. Pusha just wanted to put work in for the hood. But all I saw was vengeance from Glizzy, which I understood. No matter the motives we were ready to go up on the scoreboard.

We sped our pace up as soon as the house came into view. All of them suckaz were still posted on the porch talking loud and having the time of their lives. They were lackin' fo'real. We got halfway across the street before one of the suckaz spotted us. But it was too late, we were in Kobe range.

"Jump me now cuz!" Glizzy screamed then started the show.

BLOC! BLOC! BLOC! BOOM! BOOM! BOOM! BOOM!

The nigga that spotted us made it inside the house, but the one behind him took a few slugs to the back. He dropped before he could make it inside. Two of his homies decided to let their nutz hang and bust back on us. All I could see was a fire blazing the night from all angels and moving shadows. I kept the heat aimed at the porch with my trigga finger in overdrive.

"Fuck Gas Team, nigga!" a sucka yelled as he threw some hot shit our way.

It was a full-fledged shootout now, three vs two. The enemies had the advantage though since they had the porch for a shield.

BOC! BOC! BOC! BOOM! BOOM! BOOM!

I started walking backwards letting my slugs fly as I shielded myself behind a car. I'd be damned if I stood in the middle of the street just waiting to get gunned down like a muthafuckin' dummy.

YOPPA! YOPPA! YOPPA! YOPPA! YOPPA

The sound of a choppa roaring in the night made every other sound come to a halt. All I heard was metal being sliced through like butter as those bullets ripped through parked cars. I peeped around the car.

"Y'all bitches shot my brother!" The one that ran into the house had come back out bustin' with a vengeance. YOPPA! YOPPA! YOPPA!

He stood on the edge of the car waving that big muthafucka side to side like the terminator. *Ah hell naw!* "We gon' shoot while we run back to the car," I told the homies who were ducking behind a car right next to

mine.

"Let's do this shit!" Pusha yelled back.

I waited a few seconds then popped up letting my hammer bang at those pussies. The homies started firing right after me. We took 'em by surprise. They started backing up while we made our way up out of there.

BOOM! BOOM! BOOM! BOC! BOC! YOPPA! YOPPA! YOPPA!

Soon as we made it to the corner, we took off like track stars. I didn't exhale until we hopped in and peeled out safely. My heart was pounding heavily, but I felt alive! I'd forgotten how much I loved the rush that came only from a shootout.

"Whoever that nigga was on the ground never got back up. Bitch ass nigga." Pusha broke the silence.

"He was the nigga with the choppa brother, fuck both of 'em. I wanted to hit that wheenie man-man so muthafuckin' bad. He was there in the mall. I'ma kill him." Glizzy vented.

"Every score counts lil' bro. Every time we make the suckaz shed a tear it's a celebration for us. This shit gon' last for a little minute. We gon' have more than enough time to catch all of 'em. Don't get too anxious, that's how you make mistakes that'll get you killed." I dropped game.

Chapter 11
Jamar

We were riding in silence until Glizzy shouted out of nowhere. "Cuz there goes that nigga Ace!" He pointed across the street.

My heart skipped a beat. Lo and behold, there was ace all by himself walking out of seven-eleven. I looked around Fessenden street for any cops or witnesses. It was a plaid pantry right across the street that usually had a lot of traffic. The coast was clear. I couldn't believe he had the arrogance to be out by himself and talking on the phone. He was used to being treated like the king of the north.

"He ain't heard about his homies yet," Pusha said.

I parked on the street right next to the lot, my eyes never leaving his body. I checked my clip. *One bullet.* "I'm out, fuck!" I vented.

"Me too." Added Pusha.

"I got three bullets left. Glizzy said.

I shook my head in disbelief. We finally had one of their main niggaz that we been wanting and couldn't even capitalize.

"If it's meant to be, we'll catch 'em another time." I was sick just watching him slow stroll across the lot. "Naw, I'm killin' this nigga right now," Glizzy said then bounced out before I could stop him.

"This dummy gon' fuck round and die tryna be Wayne perry and shit."

"Who Wayne perry?"

I stared out the window instead of answering the dumb-ass question. I could barely breathe as I watched lil' bruh creep through the lot. With every step he took, I got more anxious.

"If he turns around, Glizzy dead," Pusha stated the obvious.

He was more than right. Lil' bruh wasn't close enough to survive a firefight with only three bullets. Luckily Ace was still on the phone instead of being focused on his surroundings. Not even a second later had passed from my thoughts then he hung the phone up tucking it in his pocket. *Fuck!*

"Shoot this in the air when I tell you." I tossed the gun as I slowly drove off.

"In the air?"

"Just do what I say."

Ace was almost in his car and Glizzy still wasn't close enough. Most niggaz looked around before they hopped in their whips. I couldn't let that happen. I waited until I was right in his line of sight before I stopped the car then rolled the window down.

"Fuck the goonies nigga!" I screamed out.

Ace stopped dead in his tracks. His hand shot straight to his waist like every street niggaz did when it was reppin' time. "Bust," I told Pusha.

BOOM!

He shot a cloud. We yelled 'Gas Team' then skirted out like some real suckaz. I peeped the rear-view mirror and saw him holding his arms in the air taunting us to come back.

BOOM!

Then his body crumbled to the pavement. I hurried up and busted a U-turn. Glizzy was standing over him having a conversation when we pulled up. His pistol was aimed at his face, but ace didn't give a fuck.

"Pull the trigga, ho ass nigga! That shit only gon' make me a legend." He spit a blob of blood on Glizzy.

We stared in silence at his bravery. I was so mad I was debating on getting out and killing him myself. Glizzy didn't even flinch.

BOOM! BOOM! CLICK! CLICK!

His top flew off and lil' bruh was still tryna yank him. I smiled at my goon bodying them and hit the horn.

"How you feel cuz" It had been five minutes since we fled the scene. The car was dead silent the whole time while we prayed, we made it out of the north side while we looked around for the pigs.

"That pussy spit on me," He looked at his chest for the first time and looked like he got even madder. "He lucky I ain't have more bullets cuz."

"We gotta get you out of town."

"What? Fuck naw! I ain't going nowhere.

"You gon' be too hot lil' bruh. Muthafuckaz gon' start putting pieces together then have yo name all over Facebook. You gotta lay low.

"I don't give a fuck about none of that." He dismissed everything I said with a wave of his hand. *everybody wanna be tough.* "You don't wanna die in jail cuz, I'm telling you."

"Never planned on it. I'm holding court in the streets, on Crip."
"You'll die in the streets." I shot back.

"It'll only make me a legend." He quoted a dead man.

He smiled for the first time all day. He and Pusha shook up in celebration so I decided to kill the convo, it was pointless. I let them bask in their glory. I knew they didn't know any better. Plus, I wasn't buying that whole hold court in the streets either. Everybody said that 'til a hundred cops had their guns pointed at their heads. The yards were full of killaz that swore to hold court in the streets.

Chapter 12
Juice
A Month Later

"I don't know why you still chasing this punk ass bitch anyways. She already chose her side blood." Gunna complained from the passenger seat.

I turned G-Herbo down. "You doing too much cryin' in this foreign, my nigga. In this foreign ride, let it go," I quoted Tory Lanez.

He turned his head with a crazy-ass look on his face. "Nigga, what? I'll piss in this punk ass Bentley then slap the fuck out yo bitch ass. In that order too."

Now I looked at him like he'd lost his damn mind. I screwed my face up then pointed at it like Mike Epps did. I called his bluff.

"Aight nigga, on bloods." He unbuckled his belt then unzipped his pants.

"Aye nigga!! I don't do that funny shit!" I leaned all the way over against the door.

I grabbed my heat and pointed it at his chest. "I'ma push yo shit back if you pull that lil' muthafucka out."

The car was silent for a few seconds then he leaned over with a smirk on his face. "I taught you better than that." He gripped the gun then lifted it from his chest to his head.

"I just wanted to give yo ugly ass mama an open casket," I shot back.

"Fuck you and that bitch." He blew a kiss then started laughing.

"Gay ass nigga." I drove off after missing the light a few times.

I started laughing too for no reason. We were fucked up in the head fo'sho'. But we deserved to laugh and smile. Over the past month, since those suckaz shot my truck up with my daughter inside, I'd been stacking my paper and doing my homework. I wanted to go on a murder spree starting that night, but O-Dawg talked me out of it.

CLICK! CLICK!

"You hear that shit? That's that fifty-round drum I just put in the Draco. I'm hitting a nigga with every single bullet, on my dead brother's grave," I spat.

CLICK! CLACK!

I popped a banana clip in an AK. I was sitting on the edge of my bed loading up every gun I had in my spot, which was over a dozen. Tears were dropping from my eyes at a rapid pace that I couldn't control. Through my teary vision, I saw Brittney standing in the corner looking at me. She was scared to death.

"Yeah, I hear you, lil' bruh. Now, I need you to hear me for a minute," O-Dawg said.

"Hear what? It sounds like you 'bout to start preaching that peaceful shit. I can hear it in yo voice," I spat while I loaded up my gauge.

"Fuck peace, we gon' kill any and everybody that was involved. But the problem is, we don't know who did it."

"My enemies did it and they all gon' pay for it with their blood. All of them niggaz!" I wiped away the tears of anger. They were a sign of weakness.

"They want you to go crazy and shoot everything up in sight. And as soon as one of those nobody ass niggaz that's standing outside snitch on you, then what? You gon' be in the bounty mad at the world, trust me on that one. Don't get all out of character and making emotional decisions. You can't even run right now, blood. You got responsibilities now. A team to feed and two daughters that need you."

I exhaled my frustration. I knew he was right, but I needed to put somebody in a body bag. They disrespected the fuck out of my 'G', and I had to pay 'em back. Brittney came over and laid her head on my shoulder. I looked into her eyes and knew what she wanted me to do.

"Aight big bruh, what you got planned?"

My team and I took off like a muthafuckin' rocket. Jaxx started dropping the bricks off on us by the dozens and we moved 'em just as fast with no problems. We had niggaz coppin' from us from Seattle, Vegas, and Oakland. The dope we had was shitting on everybody's in the town. It wasn't even close. In only a month our lives had changed drastically, and we had no plans on ever going back. I copped a coke white Bentley and moved Brittney and my daughter out to Salem in a four-bedroom crib. With my family living forty-five minutes from the town, it was easier to sleep at night. I was gon' give Latoya some bread to move but changed my mind when I thought of her ho ass nigga. I wish I would pay for the next man to live lavish.

"C'mon, let's get this romantic shit out the way 'cause I got shit to do," Gunna complained as he hopped out.

"Hater," I said out loud then texted Naughty letting her know I was here.

We'd been in constant contact for weeks but hadn't found the time to link up. I still felt some type of way that she was back fuckin' with her baby dad, but I could fuck on her whenever I wanted so I just chopped it up to the game. Plus, with me not living with her anymore, my baby mama drama went down to an all-time low. She was still my bitch; I was just letting him borrow her for a moment.

I hopped out of the Bentley feeling like the richest nigga in the town. I wasn't even close to a millionaire but from the looks of it, nobody could tell. The sun was hitting all my diamonds in the right places had me sparkling like a muthafucka. I had on my brotha's chain, my M.G. piece, and a dead ass Pistol Pete's chain. And if that wasn't enough, then all the diamonds that were dancing in the rollie definitely were.

I was finally able to move around without crutches and I vowed to never use a pair again. Fuck that! If the opposition ever got the drop on me again, I was gon' force them to put a bullet in my dome. No matter the odds I was gon' squeeze the trigga until I was dead and gone. My worse fear wasn't death, unlike most of these scary-ass niggaz out here perpetrating this gangsta shit that really flows through my veins. But I did fear being paralyzed in a wheelchair for the rest of my life. Fuck that! I'd rather die. Being on crutches really fucked with my mental.

"You ready, fake ass pretty boy?" JoJo said as he walked over with Ghost and Black following behind him.

They were trailing us the whole ride over just in case shit got real. "You really putting it on thick for sis huh?" He laughed.

I sucked my teeth. "Nigga this me, is that you? I wish I would go out my way to impress any bitch." I fronted.

They all looked at me like they knew I was lying through my teeth. I waved them hating ass niggaz away then started walking through the lot. They started snickering behind my back. My eye scanned the whole lot for any sign of beef. The shopping center her shit was in had hella businesses in it, so it was highly likely that we'd bump into somebody. The twin .45's on my waist boosted my confidence though, plus I had a pack of savages walking behind me that hoped we had to kill somebody.

Once we got a few feet away we could see inside the whole store. Jessie saw me first then faith locked her gold-digging eyes on us. I saw Naughty hanging some clothes on a wall. They must have said something to her cause she instantly snapped her neck in my direction. We locked eyes and for a split second, it felt like the whole world had frozen. All I could see was her and all she could see was me. A wave of emotions rushed through my body out of nowhere and I didn't like the shit. I put an extra pep in my step then turned my head breaking our connection. I looked around like I was scanning the lot.

"Hey, Papi Juice!" Jessie yelled when we walked in the room. "What's good Miami?" I replied.

"Bitch what I tell you 'bout that Papi shit?" Naughty checked her then rolled her eyes.

"He ain't yo man no more, might as well let me have 'em," She flipped her off. "I love your new Bentley. When you gon' let me borrow it?" She kept fucking with Naughty.

"Soon as I cop another one."

She sped past Naughty and came over and hugged me extra tight. She was being hella dramatic on purpose to get under Naughty's skin.

I decided to play along for the fuck of it. I wanted to see how much she still loved me. I gripped Jessie around the waist then put my nose in her neck. "Damn, you smell good," I said loud enough for Naughty to hear. I kept my eyes on her to witness the jealousy.

It didn't take long at all. She marched over like an angry rhino ready to kill both of us.

Y'all keep fuckin' around and I'ma stab both of y'all through the neck and I'm not playing!"

I brushed Jessie off me while I busted out laughing from the look on Naughty's face. She had her fists balled up ready to take off on both of us. I snatched her ass up before she could hit me. I wrapped her ass up tight then whispered in her ear. "I miss you, baby," then kissed her neck a few times. I felt her body melt into mine. My hands found their way to her ass palming it. "I love you, baby, fo'real."

She wrapped her arms around my neck." I love you too." She looked me in the eyes then stuck her tongue in my mouth.

"Y'all gon' get a room or what?" JoJo hated from the sideline. "You know yo brother here, right? You can at least act like you care, shit!"

"Aww, my baby brother jealous." She let go of me then approached him. "Give big sis a hug." She tried to wrap him up.

"Bitch please." He stiffed armed her like a running back. "I see exactly who I want a hug from." He licked his lips as he made his way over to Faith.

"Boy, I done told yo young ass a hundred times that we're like family." She held her arm out in an attempt to stop him.

"And I done told you," He grabbed her arm and snatched her up with ease. "We belong together." He tried to tongue her down, but she fought him off and escaped his grasp.

"Girl, get yo brother before I fuck him up!" she yelled at Naughty as she walked over to us.

SMACK!

JoJo smacked her ass then gripped it. "I knew that juicy muthafucka was soft."

"That's gon' cost you nigga!"

He sucked his teeth then pulled out a stack. She turned her gold-digging ass right around. Then he pulled an even bigger knot from his other pocket. Lil' bruh had at least ten bands on 'em.

"I keep telling you I really do this shit. I ain't no little nigga no more, this grown man business right here. So whatever nigga you got yo eyes on just know he ain't gon' last long. We killin' all the competition off, so you better hurry up and chose while I'm interested."

"Boy bye." She stuck her hand out.

He handed over a bill. She put her hand on her hips then rolled her neck with an attitude. He forked over another bill like a true trick. She walked off without saying a word. SMACK! He smacked her ass again with a smile on his face. We all started laughing at his trickin' ass. Faith kept walking this time fronting like she ain't like the attention.

"Hey y'all," She greeted the rest of us. "Wassup bro?" Then she hugged me.

Bitch never hugged me before. I was slightly thrown off but hugged her back. When I let go and looked her in the eyes is when I understood what the attitude change was about. The dollar signs were in her eyes. She'd been hating on me for years and now she had the audacity to be starry-eyed and shit.

"Shit what's good? How you living?" I played along with her.

I'm straight," She grabbed the chain that used to hang from bitch ass Pistol Pete's neck. "I like this chain." She had a smile on her face.

Naughty looked at the chain then at Faith's smile confused. She knew exactly who used to own the muthafucka. The whole town did. But what she didn't know was that faith was the one that set him up.

"C'mon baby, let me show you around the store. I need to get you away from these thirsty ass bitches." She grabbed my hand pulling me away.

"Oh, now he baby? That ain't what you was saying the other day, fake bitch." Jessie said. Naughty flipped her off. "Go suck on Gunna dick."

"Yea dat. "Gunna added...

Naughty showed me around the store for ten minutes pointing out everything as we walked. Her face lit up every time she showed me some clothes or told me how much she paid for them compared to how much she would sell them for. A wave of guilt hit me. *I should have bought this for her.* Her passion mixed with her happiness convicted my conscience. I never knew she was that serious about owning her own business and getting out of the club. Or maybe I did and just didn't care.

"What's back there?" I pointed to a hallway at the back of the shop. "Bathroom and my office."

"Office huh? You bossing up, let me see it."

"It ain't much but it's mine," she said then let me in the room.

It was small but well put together. I closed the door then locked it. "Nice office, I like it." I had a smirk on my face.

"Umm-hmm, what you lock the door for?" She raised her eyebrows with her arms folded. "So, we can talk, I got some shit to get off my chest."

"You need the door locked to talk?

I pulled her into my chest. We just stood there rocking back and forth for a few seconds taking each other in. I pushed my gangsta to the side for a minute.

"I'm sorry baby." I stared her dead in the eyes so she could see my sincerity. "For what?"

"For not taking your future as seriously as I should of. For mistreating you instead of putting you first. For not appreciating you like I should have. For every time I made you cry, for everything. I'm sorry, I miss you like crazy, and I love you to death." I poured my heart out to her.

The tears instantly started flowing from her eyes. She never heard me apologize for shit so it must have really fucked with her emotions. All she could do was nod her head and wipe the tears.

"Don't cry baby, you know that hurts my heart." I wiped some tears then pulled her back in.

"I know," she let out a quick laugh then kissed my neck, "I do miss you though."

My dick got had instantly. I slid my hands under her skirt and started rubbing on her ass. "I know you feel that steel, you miss him too?"

"Maybe." She whispered in my ear.

"What about her?" I started playing with her clit.

"Ahh, Ahh. Stop, Juice, not right now." She moaned out.

"Shut up, this still my pussy. Now cum for me, baby." I sped my hand pace up.

"But they're all out there, even my brother."

"You said that to say what? This pussy don't seem to mind, you feel how wet you are?" I leaned her back on the desk then lifted her leg.

I stuck two fingers inside her pussy and got to finger poppin' her just like I know she liked it. Within seconds she had head tilted back while rolling hips to the beat of my fingers.

"Oh shit, I'm 'bout to cum," she moaned.

I sped it up. "Cum then, nut for a real nigga."

She covered her mouth with both hands to mute out her moaning. She was cumming.

"Ohh, ohh! Ahhh!"

"You good? I asked with a smirk on my face.

She nodded. I pulled my fingers out then sucked her juices off them.

"you still taste sweet." I stuck them in her mouth to give her a taste.

After she sucked them dry, I pulled the pistols from my waist and dropped them on her desk. Then yanked my pants down to the floor. My dick stood at attention ready to dive inside of her. She grabbed it then started stroking it.

"We can't fuck right now baby, it's not enough time."

"Stop talkin' and turn around so I can hit this."

I flipped her around then pushed her over the desk. I pulled her thong to the side then slid right up in her tight ass pussy. *Got Damn!* I hadn't piped her down in months and forgotten how tight and wet her shit was. I was ready to blast off instantly. Naughty gripped the edge of the desk for support then started backing her fat ass up against me.

"Cum daddy! Ahh! Ahh!" She was going crazy tryna get me to nut in a hurry.

I watched her ass clap against my stomach in amazement then slapped it. *SMACK!*

"This still my pussy bitch?"

"Yes, daddy!"

I grabbed her cakes stopping her from throwing it back. I was ready to let loose. I was gon' pull out and bust on her cheeks but changed my mind at the last second. "Agg, Agghh!" I shot a heavy load of nut inside of her while I leaned on her back.

"Whew," I exhaled in her ear. "I almost forgot you got some fuckin' fire."

"You think my brother heard us?"

"I'm thinking about putting it in yo ass."

I ignored her question not giving a fuck if he did.

"Oh, hell naw, get off of me boy." She started tryna wrestle me off her.

I pinned her down easily. "Stop moving, I'm tryna make every second count inside this pussy." I grinded on her ass while kissing her neck.

Soon as I started getting hard again somebody knocked on the door. "What's good!?" I yelled out.

"Jamar just pulled up!" Jessie yelled back. "Oh shit! Get off me!" Naughty yelled.

I pulled out then watched her panic like the feds were 'bout to raid the drug house. I calmly put myself back together like I did every morning.

"Hurry up Juice! shit." She flashed while double-checking her appearance.

I grabbed the twin .45's and let 'em hang by my legs. I'd be damned if I was gonna walk out unprepared for the worse. *Fuck That!*

"Can you put those up? I don't want you to kill my sons' father." She begged for the next nigga low key pissing me off.

"I'ma tell you one time and one time only, so pay attention. You better control yo nigga or he gon' die in yo arms." I growled then walked out on her.

My niggaz were posted in the corner with their guns out ready for war. None of them seemed to be concerned about the triv at all. It would just be another sucka for love laid out on the pavement bleeding from his head. Just another day.

"He just been sitting there, we're not sure if he saw yo car or not," Gunna told me.

"How y'all wanna play it?" I asked the gang.

"Blood, let's just shake. I would hate to be in jail for smoking my nephew's dad. I stopped by real quick to see my sister's shop and y'all met me up here." JoJo came up with the game plan.

Naughty nodded her approval while the other two looked scared to death. I always found it funny how bitches loved to fuck with street niggaz and talk that ride or die shit then fold up at the first opportunity. But I knew a lot of niggaz that did too so fuck it.

"Whatever we gon' do, let's hurry up and do it because he might have spotted yo whip and called for backup," Gunna added.

"Well, he better stay in the car 'til they get here then. C'mon, let's blow this joint." I tucked my heats then walked out.

We didn't get five steps before Jamar and his main nigga Flip and some lil nigga that looked familiar hopped out. Jamar sucka ass had an arm full of roses and a smile on his face. *I just fucked yo bitch.* I guess he came to surprise the love of his life and show her his appreciation. Once Jamar locked eyes with me his facial expression went from happy to confused to pure hatred instantly. Flip hand shot straight to his waist and so did ours. The roses hit the ground as Jamar reached for his too. His lil nigga was the only one that ain't reach.

"Y'all pull them pistols out and we gon' leave y'all thoughts all over this parking lot," I growled.

I didn't wanna catch three bodies right across the street from the police precinct in broad day, but if I had to choose between their mothers crying or mine, I chose theirs.

Jamar looked from me to JoJo then past us which told me the bitches were behind us. He looked like he'd just been betrayed, which he did.

"I don't do good with threats cuz." Flip spat.

I shrugged my shoulders. "I don't make 'em, I make promises."

"Cuz fuck all that shit! What the fuck you up here doing at my shop? Didn't I tell you to stay away from my family? Huh?! Jamar let his emotions get the best of him.

I smiled at him. "Nigga I don't answer questions from cops or suckaz. So, either bust that little ass pistol on yo waist or shut the fuck up and pick those flowers up and give "em to yo bitch."

I eased the twins slightly off my waist ready to get it poppin'. I was done talking and damn sho' wasn't feeling his tone. He tried yelling at me like I was his bitch or something. I saw him bite on his lip then his hand inch closer to his heat. I wasn't worried though. He would never get it out before I filled him up with some hot shit!

"Hold up blood, Jamar chill out!" JoJo said then stepped in between our crews. "I came up here to see sis and check the shop out. I had the homies meet me up here when they banged my line."

Jamar nodded along like he was really buying the shit. But I knew he was just fronting in order to live another day.

"And I told yo ass not to ever have this nigga around, period!" He yelled and pointed at Naughty.

I started walking off once he directed his anger at his baby mama. I had better things to do than to be arguing in a parking lot over some pussy that my nut was still squirming inside of.

"Aye blood, spit that shit from that one song," Gunna demanded.

I stopped dead in my tracks. Now I knew why he looked so familiar to me. We'd been waiting to catch up with his ho ass. *Pusha.*

"What cuz?" Pusha poked his chest out.

"You know what the fuck I'm talking about, oh rappin' ass nigga! You had my hood all in yo mouth when you dropped that diss track on the Goonies. So, spit that shit now." Gunna got all up in his grill.

"What the fuck I look like? A rapper on demand?" He held his ground.

"Naw, you look like a scary-ass crab to me. Matter of fact, I need that!" WHAP!

Gunna connected with his jaw sitting him on his ass instantly.

Me, JoJo, Black and Ghost yanked out and had then thangs pointed at Flip and Jamar's domes before they could even think of reaching.

"Hold up cuz! Let the homie get up and catch the fair one." Jamar stood in front of Gunna with his hand on his chest.

I kept my eyes on Flip. I could see the fire in his eyes and knew he wanted to start shooting so bad. I knew at that moment we were gon' have to get him out the way first when the war popped off. We locked eyes before I could finish my thought. He smiled at me then nodded his head in understanding. *He gon' be a problem*. He knew we had this one and had already started planning their get back. If we were anywhere else in the town, I would have crushed him with no hesitation.

"That's all yo got lil" nigga?" Gunna wiped some blood from his mouth.

They were going at it like a muthafucka. Pusha was holding his own to my surprise. But I knew he fucked up the moment he wrapped Gunna up. Gunna was hella strong and wrestling was his specialty. He did exactly what I'd seen him do a hundred times. He dipped low, grabbed Pusha by the legs then he was airborne.

SMACK!

The crunching sounds of the bodies crashing into the concrete was sickening. Fight over. "Yea bitch! Rap that crab shit now!" Gunna stood over him like Ali did Frazier.

"I'ma kill you, nigga!" Pusha vowed from the ground.

"What's good cuz? Let me get my ones real quick." Jamar put his hands up like a boxer. I screwed my face up not believing what the fuck he'd just said.

He smirked at me. "What, you scared to fight?" He taunted.

"You wanna fight for yo life in the hospital? I don't box, I bury niggaz." I kept it a hunnid.

I had no intentions of fighting no love-struck, buff ass nigga fresh out the pen. All them niggaz do is fight and lift weights in there. I did drugs and counted money all day, so wasn't no way I was in shape to catch a fade with him. Fuck that!

"I called the cops! They're on the way!" an old white lady yelled at us.

I looked around and noticed a dozen white people staring at us. A few of them were on the phone no doubt calling the pigs.

"You better pull that trigga if you wanna live long. Better to do life in the pen than the ground." Flip held his arms out daring me to shoot.

I kicked the flowers on the ground just to fuck with Jamar then broke into the car.

Chapter 13
Juice

"Boom! You see how hard I slammed his bitch ass!? I bet he somewhere trying on a back brace right now." Gunna yelled being hella extra like always.

It had been hours since the triv with them Gas Team niggaz and we still hadn't stopped talking about it. Every time a new homie popped up at JoJo's spot, we had to break it all down again, play by play. After we peeled out, we came straight to his spot to plot out the next few moves. He owed me a hunnid bands from the last load I fronted him and had it all together for me, so coming to his spot was already in the plans. He called his team and I called mine. Now everybody was there except Mask. He had to go grab ten bricks from the stash spot for JoJo.

"Play that part back again. I wanna see dawg face again while he goes airborne," Twin said.

It was at least fifteen of us standing in the front room staring at the sixty-inch tv screen. I didn't even notice Black recording the whole triv from the moment Gunna pushed up on Pusha. The video had the net going crazy plus my phone was off the hook. Even o-dawg hit my line laughing about the shit.

I sat on the couch and let my mind wander while the gang was busy laughing and joking at the suckaz. I kept picturing Flip's face and the fire in his eyes. I knew that look all too familiar. We needed to be ready 'when' those niggaz struck back, not 'if they did. It wasn't a doubt in my heart that they were coming, and Flip would be on the front line.

They were fucking the goonies up, so I had no choice but to respect their gangsta. They'd dropped like five of those pussies in the last month and hadn't lost one nigga. After they bodied Ace, they put the streets on notice and hadn't taken their feet off their necks. They were deep with Crips and Bloods and had their money up. I wasn't gon' be the one to sleep on them just because we got one up on them.

"Yo Juice? Why you ask that nigga did he wanna fight for his life? That's the best part of the whole video." Shooter, one of JoJo homies said.

"Naw, my shit was when you kicked the flowers. That shit was epic, on gang," Flash added.

I nodded at both of them then went back to plotting on my newest enemies. I realized I didn't have any lines on any of them except Jamar. I didn't know who their baby mamas were or their side bitches, who they got money with, or where they hung out the most. All I knew was that they were known for clubbing hard and buying the bars out. And ray-ray and d-roc were supposedly millionaires that were barely seen anymore.

"Y'all see what happened to the last niggaz that posted a video on them right?! They slept on their gangstaz and now a few of them are sleep forever!" I hopped up and broke up their little victory lap.

"Well, we ain't the last niggaz and we damn sho' don't sleep on nobody," TJ just always had to be the one to defy me. "And I'm not too impressed with their g's either, have you seen this video?"

"Fuck that video! Y'all in here celebrating like we just won the muthafuckin' super bowl. Watch their body count, not the video when we had the drop on 'em." I got up in his face with the facts.

I saw it in his eyes that he wasn't feeling me evading his space. But I didn't give a fuck though. I wasn't feeling how he always had something smart to say like he was challenging my authority. Ever since I got the plug, he'd been acting weird towards me. But doing that shit in front of other niggaz really had me feeling some type of way. I couldn't expect respect from the drama gang if my own homie didn't give me his. The whole room got silent at our stare down.

"What's good, gang?!" Mask shouted from behind me.

I turned around and saw brody all smiles and shit with a duffle bag hanging from his arm. Omar closed the door then handed him the wood he'd been smoking on.

"Just in time for the bullshit," Omar said.

Mask started shaking everybody up making his way through the crowd.

"On the gang, that shit funny as a muthafucka. Fuck them niggaz," He pointed at the screen which was still on Facebook playing the video. Then he shook up TJ before giving me a g-hug. "Not right now bro, let it go." He whispered in my ear.

We locked eyes and for a split second, I could hear everything he wanted to say to me. He didn't even know what the triv was about but didn't want us beefing in front of other niggaz. I gave him a quick nod then walked off. *I'ma check this nigga later.*

"Is my drama gang niggaz ready to get a bag or what?!" He started dumping bricks on the table.

They rushed over to grab one, knocking each other over in the process totally forgetting about our little situation. JoJo nodded at me for me to follow him down the hall. I gave Omar the sign to follow me. We followed him to his room upstairs away from everybody else which is what I needed. I was still mad as fuck and had to block out thoughts of murdering TJ.

"You good nigga?" JoJo grabbed a duffle bag from the closet and handed it over.

I didn't even open it, there was no need to. I handed it to Omar then sat on the edge of the bed. I ran my hands through my dreads then exhaled my frustration.

"Call yo sis real quick, check on her."

"I wish that nigga would," He screwed his face up then called her. "She hit ignore," he said seconds later.

"Try again."

"She ignored me again, punk bitch." He stared at the phone in disbelief.

I almost broke his jaw for disrespecting my bitch like that. I had to remind myself that she was his blood sister and that's how they talked to each other. *Chill out Juice.* My anger was building up inside of me and was dying to get taken out on somebody.

"You know You're the only nigga that can get away with, disrespecting her like that."

He turned his neck and looked at me crazy. "I feel the same exact way about you." He shot back.

"My lil' bruh." I shook him up to kill whatever Lil' tension.

"If shit hit the fan, sis gon' have to choose sides. We putting her in a bad spot."

"Ain't no ifs, we definitely going to war so make sure yo team ready. We can't play with them at all, real shit."

"Yo Juice! JoJo! Omar!" I heard Gunna yell out.

My hand went straight to the pistol on my waist then I opened the door. I knew when Gunna was mad, and it was all in his voice. He was standing at the bottom of the stairs looking like one of Satan's fallen soldiers. I put my arms in the air.

"Y'all come see this shit, blood! I know who almost shot yo daughter!" he roared and then disappeared. I flew down the stairs three at a time.

Chapter 14
Juice

"Show 'em how we figured it out," Gunna told Ghost, who was controlling the Facebook from his phone that was connected to the TV.

I really didn't give a fuck how they put it together, I just wanted to know who did it. But I didn't wanna step over my nigga's commands or miss out on important information. So instead of speaking, I walked closer to the TV and stared at it. All I saw was a bunch of comments about the video.

"This is Lil Teflon right here with his bitch ass," Ghost said then blew up his post. "Juice was scared to run cuz his fade. I wonder why? Once again, his bodyguard Gunna turnt up and saved him. That's twice!" he read it word for word.

I shrugged my shoulders. "They usually say Omar's my bodyguard."

"Why would some little nobody ass nigga that we don't know say that's twice?" Gunna pointed out.

"Don't know."

"Tell me if he looks familiar."

Ghost went to his page and clicked on his picture, blowing it up. I recognized him instantly. I stepped closer and stared at him with pure hate. He was the nigga that tried to kill me with my daughter. *That's yo ass.*

"I'm crushin' that nigga, on my brotha's grave," I growled my vow.

"Hold up, blood. It gets better."

Another picture popped up, this time with another young nigga and they were throwing their hood up. I recognized his bitch ass too.

"What's his name?" I asked the room.

"Dirty. He and Lil Teflon are from Murk Unit, my enemies. Lil Teflon is Teflon's younger brother, he's like fifteen," JoJo said.

"I'm killin' 'em both," Omar jumped in.

I was more confused than ever. I'd never killed or robbed anybody from their section, so I was lost on their desire to put me in a coffin. Only one solution ran through my mind.

"They got at me 'cause we fuck with y'all?" I asked JoJo. That's how it goes in the streets, so I wasn't surprised at all.

He shrugged his shoulders not knowing what to say.

"Naw, look at this shit right here. This Teflon's page," Ghost said.

A post from over a month ago was on the screen. I read it out loud, "Damn brody, they got to you. Gang almost had 'em. R.1.P. Pistol Pete." I was seeing red now.

"He posted that the next morning after ol' boy died. The day after they tried us," Gunna pointed out.

"Pete's ho ass paid them to kill me. I should go bury his scary ass up and shoot him myself this time. Fuckin' pussy." I held his chain up with an evil smirk on my face. "We got a lot of suckaz to kill, I hope y'all ready."

Chapter 15
Naughty

"I'm surprised he ain't whoop yo ass, I know I would have. You a thot fo'real, fuckin' a nigga in the shop yo baby daddy bought for you." Faith had the audacity to say.

It was the day after all the drama went down and it was me, her, and Jessie sitting in my living room. They came over hella early to make sure I was coo'. I was beyond stressed out!

"I know. All he did was come home to grab some guns then left without saying a word. I tried to talk to him, but he acted like I didn't even exist. I've never seen him that mad before, he looked like a demon."

"Damn Naughty what you gon' do?" Jessie asked.

"I don't know, girl, just wait til he's ready to talk. That's all I can do."

"No, I mean with all the niggaz in yo life beefing with each other. You got yo side nigga and yo brother teamed up against yo baby dad aka yo main nigga. You better figure it out."

Little did she know, but I stayed up all night trying to figure everything out. I played every scenario in my head repeatedly until I fell to sleep.

"Y'all really think it's gon' get that bad? Cause niggaz talk shit and fight all the time then nothing ever happens.

Nobody even got shot so I don't see why it's that serious." I vented.

"Bitch what?" Faith twisted her neck then gave me the stank face. "It would have been better if somebody would have got shot. A Lil' leg shot or something then maybe shit could have died down. Naw this 'bout to be some heavy shit so get ready. Somebody you love gotta die. Muthafuckaz was clowning Jamar all night and this morning about them flowers."

I hopped off the couch and started pacing back and forth. I knew she was right, but I felt like being delusional for

a minute. Being optimistic made me feel better. "AGHHHHH!" I screamed while trying to pull my hair out. I couldn't understand for the life of me why my life was always so fucking packed with drama. I really needed a

break.

"So, what are you going to do?"

"I don't fucking know what to do, Faith, shit!" I raised my voice out of frustration.

She rolled her eyes. "Well, you better figure it out real quick."

I sat back down and tried to clear my thoughts. I breathed in deep then exhaled even deeper. *Get it together.* "How would you feel if Jamar or his homies killed JoJo?" Jessie asked a dumb-ass question.

I snapped my neck in her direction so fast I'm surprised it didn't break. "I'll kill that nigga in his sleep with no hesitation. What kinda question is that?"

She stuck her hand in the air. "Just hold up, I'm tryna help you figure this shit out. How would you feel if they killed Juice?"

"I don't know what I'd do, I know I'll be sick. I still love him."

"What if he killed yo baby daddy, would you be with him? Have him around yo son?"

It took me a minute to run the scenario through my mind. It was at that moment that I fully understood the predicament I was in.

"I don't think I could be with him if he killed Jamar and he damn sure couldn't be around my son. I would be the worst mother if I did some shit like that." I concluded.

"Last question. If JoJo killed Jamar and not Juice, could you be with Juice?"

"I don't know, I really don't.

"It's obvious what you gotta do then," Faith said.

"What?"

"You're on Juice's side by default 'cause of yo brother. So, you might as well start preparing yourself for Jamar's funeral and your wedding to Juice. Oh, if Juice gets killed, then best believe JoJo ain't gon' rest until Jamar and his niggaz are dead. So, you might as well show your loyalty and set the nigga up. Secure your future for the best outcome."

I looked at Jessie to make sure she'd just heard the same craziness that I did. From the look she gave me, I knew we were on the same page. *This bitch foul.* I stared back at faith to see if she was gon' start laughing and tell me she was just playing.

She raised her eyebrows then gave me a stank face letting me know she was dead serious. She looked at me like I was the crazy one.

"Bitch you serious? Set my baby daddy up? What kinda fag shit is you on?" I grilled her.

"Fag shit? You the one just fucked your baby dad's enemy in the shop he paid for," She used her hands as quotation marks when she said baby dad. "All this shit is your fault, I'm tryna help you come out on top. Fuck Jamar, it ain't like the nigga done ever did anything for you. Hold up, let's count it up," She help up a finger for each point. "One, he ain't never been a good dad. Two, he gave you an STD five different times. Three, he used to whoop yo ass for practice. Four, he had yo dumb ass out here stripping and selling pussy on the low just to pay his lawyer fees and was cheating the whole time. He gets out and drops a few stacks for a shop and now You're Bonnie to his Clyde? Bitch please." She sucked her teeth.

I couldn't front like she wasn't telling the truth, but I still wasn't with that setup shit. I was still having nightmares about helping Juice kill Jamar and I didn't even know him. I don't know how niggaz kill each other then go to sleep like nothing happened. Fuck that!

"You would really do that?" I asked.

She sucked her teeth. "In a heartbeat, fuck the bullshit. I'd rock out with Juice cause he's definitely on the rise, all the way till he goes to jail for life. And he's definitely going in the next year or two, then I'd shake his ass."

Jessie busted out laughing. "You hella scandalous!"

"I don't give a fuck! Ain't nobody tells these niggaz to go around killing each other over everything. And Juice been crazy, it's only gon' get worse the more money he makes. I'd be over there sucking his shit right now and then do whatever he needed me to do to prove myself."

No matter what she said I couldn't see myself doing no shit like that. I wasn't setting nobody up for anybody, not even for my brother. If they were gonna shoot at each other, then that was on them. I wouldn't have anything to do about it.

"I know what I'ma do." I blurted out after a second of silence.

"What? They asked at the same time.

"I'ma talk to JoJo, make him stay out of their beef. I'ma beg him to see the position it puts me in. I can get through to him, I know it."

"Who you tryna convince, us or yourself? That nigga ain't staying out of shit and you know it." Faith shot me down.

Before I could respond to her the front door flew open and Jamar walked in. He mugged us up and down like we were the scum of the earth. His eyes were bloodshot red, and he had on the same black hoodie that he left in yesterday.

"Hey, baby?" I walked over to give him a hug.

He pushed me away then walked down the hall. I felt so embarrassed but chopped it up while following behind him.

"Can you talk to me please?"

He kept walking like I didn't exist. I followed him all the way to our bedroom then stood in the doorway, hands on my hips blocking his ass from leaving. I stared a hole through him as he switched hoodies then grabbed another gun from the closet.

"Get out my way." He growled.

"Nigga you ain't going nowhere until you talk to me!" I yelled in his face.

"I promised myself when I was in the pen that I wouldn't put my hands on you again," He bit down on his lip. I could see him tryna control his anger. "Don't make me break that promise." He picked me up and tossed me to the side like a bag of feathers.

I thought about punching him in the back of his head while he walked away. But I quickly changed my mind after I thought about how strong he was. I didn't feel like getting my ass whooped.

"I didn't do nothing Jamar! It ain't my fault they showed up with my brother."

He kept on walking, letting my words slide off his back. He didn't wanna hear shit I had to say. He stopped at the door then stared at all three of us.

"For now on, if any of y'all are caught loafing with those suckaz you won't be spared. We not gon' hesitate just cause y'all wanna get ya pussies ate. If you fuckin' with the opposition, then you can die with em," he said then walked out.

"I told you, I told you," Faith said as soon as the door slammed.

***

I pulled up to my lil brother's spot an hour later with hopes of talking him out of the beef with Jamar. The last thing I needed was for my brother to be laying up in somebody's funeral home. I'd lose my mind fo'real. I didn't know if Jamar's threat applied to JoJo or not, but I damn sho' wasn't gon' cut my brother off for nobody. *He must be crazy*. I knew I couldn't tell JoJo about that cause then he would really flip the fuck out."

"I'm outside," I said then hung up.

I had to mentally prepare myself for the conversation. He was the definition of a hot head and was known for doing the opposite of what he knew was right. I let out a few deep breaths then hopped out.

"Hey bro," I said soon as he opened the door.

"Why the fuck you kept ignoring me last night? Come here," He grabbed my chin and moved my face around until he was satisfied that I had no marks on me. "I was gon' kill that nigga today if you had a single mark on you."

"He doesn't hit me."

He screws his face up then walked inside. I followed him to the couch where his flunky Ghost was sitting. I looked at all the guns on the table.

I couldn't tell if he was gearing up for war or was about to do a deal with the cartel. Ghost nodded at me and I gave him one back. JoJo lit up a Backwood then stared at me.

"I was too young to kill that nigga back in the day for putting his hands on you, but now shit is different."

"He doesn't hit me anymore," I vowed again.

"Look, can we talk in private? I have something important to talk to you about."

"Anything you tell me I'ma tell my lil homie anyways. Plus, we already know what you came to talk about." He handed Ghost the weed then pulled me in closer.

"lift your shirt up real quick."

I was lost. "Huh? Lift my shirt up?"

"I know how them woman beaters be attacking the body to avoid facial marks and shit. So, lift your shirt or I'ma slam you on the couch then rip it off, your choice."

He was dead serious. The glare in his eyes told me not to challenge him on this one. I loved how protective over me he was, but this was a lil too much. I sucked my teeth then pulled my shirt all the way up to my bra.

"Don't be looking at me neither lil boy, over there getting hard and shit." I took my frustration out on Ghost.

He waved me off then kept playing with the big-ass gun in his hands. JoJo inspected every inch then turned me around before he was satisfied.

"The answer is no, fuck no." He pulled my shirt down then pushed me away.

"How you gon' say no before I even ask you? What kinda shit is that?" I tossed my hands on my hips and rolled my neck.

"You came to do what all bitches do that's scared and in love. You want us to fall back on yo nigga, right?"

"Wrong! I want you to fall back! Let the rest of them shoot each other, you stay out of it, Please."

They both looked at me like I was dumb.

"So, betray Juice, right? Say fuck 'em and go back on my word? Bitch I'm loyal, you need to learn what that means. Everything you see right now is cause of that nigga Juice! He put my team on and I'd rather die then turn my back on him, fuck that." He was mad as fuck now.

"Bitch, how you know Juice ain't put his hands on me?"

"He has, you're a black bitch. We have to slap y'all every now and then when y'all try us. But he's never balled up his fist and cracked your jaw!" He jumped up and yelled in my face. Even when you actually socked his ass and don't think he ain't tell me 'bout when you almost spit on him. Jamar used to hit you like you were a nigga and he gotta pay for that. Fuck that nigga!"

I started crying for some reason. "So, you don't care if your nephew grows up without a dad?"

He shrugged his shoulders. "I'm his dad, and he gon' have Juice, too. Go home and enjoy the lil time you have left with that nigga. Then you gon' mourn, then you and Juice gon' be together and you'll be thanking me. Now leave before I change my mind and lock you in the backroom."

I stared my lil brother in the eyes and no longer recognized him I finally saw him for the cold-hearted nigga that everybody said he was. He didn't even kinda care about the position he was putting me in. Now I was really hot!

POW!

I punched him hard as I could right in his chest knocking his ass back down on the couch. He started laughing like Kevin Hart was in the muthafuckin' room with us.

"Fuck you punk! And fuck Juice too! And I'm not being with him either!" I stormed off with tears dripping down my face.

"I'ma charge yo nigga for that!" JoJo yelled after me.

I could still hear him laughing all the way to the car. I sped from his house then called Faith.

"Hello?" She answered.

"You were right, he didn't give a fuck!"

Chapter 16
Juice

"Yeah, we gon' crush all of them niggaz soon as I get back from Seattle. We have been sitting on the triv for a few days letting shit die down. Those lil niggaz don't even know we know what they did. I'm personally shooting both of 'em in the head."

It had been days since the stunt at Naughty's Shop and there still hadn't been no shots let off. I'd been more focused on doing my homework on the top niggaz from Murk Unit. Those lil boys had no idea who they were really funkin' with. They were used to beefin' with teenagers who only shot at their opps when they saw them on spur of the moment situations. They didn't understand it was levels to this shit and they were downstairs. I put the phone on speaker as I hopped up to get dressed.

"As you should, fuck them wheenies blood. Just make sure you move smart cause it's a lot of money on the line. You don't wanna be in here telling stories 'bout all the cars and bitches you used to have."

I put my chains on in the mirror then felt my stomach growling from the smell of Brittney cooking breakfast.

"I'm not spending a day in prison and that's on my brother's grave. They either gon' put me in a box or leave me the fuck alone. Either way, I'm not dying in jail," I vowed

"Yeah, I hear you," his tone told me he wasn't buying it though. I didn't blame him because niggaz stayed lying about it. "Make sure you boo out in Seattle; you know I don't trust them niggaz."

"Yeah, I know gang. Look, I gotta get my day started so I'ma tap in with you when I get back in town."

"Yeah dat, plus we need to talk about you and Twin. It seems like y'all got a lil animosity still."

"Yeah a'ight, stay up." I hung up before he tried to reel me in.

I didn't have no real issue with Twin at all. It was just that he wasn't Murda Gang, and I wasn't feeling how he was forced on us. *I'm hungry as fuck.* I stepped into the kitchen ready to eat everything that baby mam cooked. I was surprised that she got up early and cooked. I came home hella late and tried to cuddle with her, but she scooted over with an attitude.

"What's up baby what you cook?" I tried to kiss her, but she moved out of the way.

"Bacon, eggs, and sausages" She answered with an attitude.

She still mad. I sat down at the table and realized I hadn't eaten with my family since I copped the house for them. I was so caught up in the streets that nothing else mattered. I knew I had to slow down but now wasn't the time. It was too many enemies to kill and way too much money to be made.

"Ashley! Come eat!" Brittney called my daughter.

Ashley walked in a minute later looking happy as hell to see me. "Hi, daddy!" She kissed me then sat down.

"Hi baby, I love you."

"Love you too"

"Here baby girl." Brittney sat down Ashley's plate then took her seat with hers.

I looked at her like she was crazy. She rolled her eyes at me.

"So, you gon' leave my food in there? You're childish for that."

"What food?" her eyebrows were raised.

I jumped up and went to the stove. To my surprise, there wasn't a single piece of bacon or nothing!

"Think about that the next time you wanna come home at four in the morning. Better go have that bitch cook you some breakfast. Got me fucked up nigga," she spat.

I held my anger in for my daughter's sake. But I was mad as fuck! How she not gon' cook for me in a house that I bought? I felt disrespected. I bit my tongue then went to the back room. I grabbed everything I needed, kissed my seed then walked out without saying a word. I knew bitches hated to be ignored so that's exactly what I did. I didn't get two blocks before she started blowing me up.

"What?" I answered.

"Get yo ass back here right now! I'm not playing with you!" she screamed in my ear.

"I'm 'bout to buy a McDonalds then eat breakfast there." I disconnected on her dumb ass.

***

It took me about forty-five minutes to drive to LaToya's spot out in Vancouver. When I pulled up, the first thing I saw was Rocky washing his lil' Beamer. His face turned sour the moment he saw the Bentley pull up. I was glad he was outside though so we could talk man to man for the first time. I was done playing games with his soft ass and now was the time that everything had to come to a breaking point. I grabbed the brown paper bag that I brought just for this situation then hopped out.

"What's good nigga?" I said as I walked up on him.

His body tensed up then he poked his chest out. "Shit you tell me?"

Stay Calm. "I wanna holla at you real quick, you good with that?" I stuck my hand out.

"Yea, what's on yo mind?" He shook my hand but looked at me hella confused.

"We ain't fucked with each other since day one for multiple reasons. But at the end of the day, neither one of us are going anywhere. You're around my daughter full time so I see no need for us to have beef."

"I never really wanted to beef with you, but I feel like you be disrespecting on the regular," he replied.

I needed my head "I have, and you pulled a gun on me and raised yo voice like I was a ho or something" He nodded along this time. "We can leave the past in the past and focus on the future. I'ma respect you like a man and you do the same. You wit' that?"

"Yeah, we good my nigga."

"Here this you," I passed him the bag. "You don't owe me nothing for that either. That's my peace offering right there."

His eyes damn near popped out of his head when he saw the kilo of coke inside of it. A smile instantly spread across his face. "Good looking nigga. You sure you don't want nothing for this?" He shook me up again like I was his new best friend.

"Naw you good, that's you. I'm 'bout to go holla at these girls, coo?"

"Hell yeah, you good." He pulled his phone out no doubt calling somebody to cop the brick from him.

Soon as I walked in Latoya was sitting at the table eating and staring at me. The smell of breakfast reminded my stomach of how hungry I was.

"what's up baby mama?" I kissed her on the forehead then sat down.

"Nigga you tell me? and don't be coming in here like we on good terms and what was in that bag you have him?" She had a major attitude with me.

I understood it though. I hadn't stopped by and checked on her or my daughter since the day my daughter almost got shot.

"I know you mad at me Toya, I fucked up big time. I don't got any excuses, but I can give you an explanation if you want?"

She folded her arms. "What you got to say for yourself? Huh?"

"I didn't wanna be around my daughter until I knew who shot at me that day and why. I couldn't look you in the eyes like a man until I knew, now I know."

"They dead yet?" she snapped.

"They won't be breathing for too much longer; their time is up."

"She was having nightmares for a week straight and you were nowhere to be found, but you had enough time to be on social media buying new Bentley's and shit."

"That shit made me feel less than a man and until I kill them the feeling ain't gon leave."

"So, your pride made you ignore your daughter's phone calls?"

"Come on toy, It ain't like that."

"Naw nigga, I wanna hear you say it. If you want my forgiveness, then swallow yo stupid ass pride and say you're sorry. Not you apologize, but you're sorry." She slapped the table out of frustration.

I exhaled. "I let my pride get in the way Latoya, I'm sorry for not being here," I told her what she wanted to hear so we could move on.

"Don't do that shit again nigga."

I nodded in agreement then pulled out the money I'd brought for her. "This for y'all, she still sleep?"

"She's at your mama house, you would know that if you called your mother sometimes."

"Yo, y'all got some of that food left? I'm hungry as fuck." I switched topics tired of the arguing.

She screwed her face up then went to the stove. "That bright light bitch don't feed you?"

"She mad I came home late, so she only cooked for her and Ashley."

She busted out laughing. "I know you flipped out!"

"Naw, I just walked out on her without saying shit. I don't got time for all that shit. I got way too much going on in the streets to be beefing at the house."

She brought me a plate over and I instantly started smashing it out. When I looked up, she was sitting there staring at me. I went right back to eating.

"What was in that bag to make him not come in here trippin?" she asked.

"I squashed the beef with 'em and give 'em a brick to get his money right."

"What?! I don't want that nigga owing you that much money Juice. He be fuckin' up too much then you gon' really wanna kill him." She flashed.

I waved her off. "I gave it to him for free, he good."

"For free?" She gave me a skeptical look.

"That lil brick ain't shit to me. I can't afford to have an enemy living around my daughter. Sooner or later, he would have ended up giving the suckaz the drop on me. but fuck all that," I stood up to leave. "I gotta go get a bag in Seattle, I'll come to see Lisa in a few days." I gave her a quick kiss then left.

Chapter 17
Jamar

"When I was the one on video making the hood look bad, niggaz sho' had a lot to say. My gangsta was being questioned like a mutha-fucka. Then what I do? Went and dropped one of their main niggaz and they still stick about it! Niggaz was talkin' all that you gotta be ready to die for the hood shit but from the video I saw, I didn't see none of that." Glizzy said then sat back down on the couch with a cold smirk on his face.

He looked right at Flip knowing he'd just killed him with his own words. Glizzy had really started to lose his mind ever since he bodied Ace. Killing somebody powerful always fucked with a nig-gaz mental, especially when they're young. Lil bruh had been on a suicide mission ever since that night. He let the whole world know on social media that he was responsible for it. He had to be averag-ing two shootings a day and didn't show any signs of slowing down either. The shit was real. Ray-Ray and D-Roc called a meeting at Ray-Ray's house to discuss how we were gonna move forward.

"The difference is," Flip slowly stood up with a scowl on his face. "You were in the mall where you knew those niggaz wasn't gon' shoot and you still ran like a bitch."

The challenge had been issued.

"Naw the difference is," Glizzy stood up now.

"You had a gun in yo hand and was scared to bust yo' thang. You weren't ready to die, like you claimed. You were a straight bitch."

"Keep talkin' and you gon' end up in a box lil weak ass nigga." Flip spat, then took a few steps closer.

"you said that to say what? It ain't nothing but space cuz." Glizzy gripped the pistol on his hip.

"Blood y'all niggaz better fall back," Ray-Ray stood in between them. "Focus all that attention on all the new enemies we got."

They stared each other down then went back to their seats. But from the looks on their faces, I already knew the shit wasn't over.

Lions and wolves didn't settle tension with a few words. We all looked at each other and shook our heads.

"All y'all niggaz are disappointing me," D-roc spoke up for the first time. He'd been sitting on the pool table stacking up kilos in multiple piles. "We put this shit together so we could sit on the top ad get money. We had to shoot our way to the top, and now y'all niggaz been doing all these shootings for what? Over what a broke nigga said on Facebook? Now it's over a bitch? Now we gotta put everything on the line cause J-money and some fake ass jack boy turned D-boy, don't fuck with each other over a striper?"

"My baby mama," I interrupted him. I wasn't feeling how he kept calling her out her name either, but I let it go." And it's not over her, it's about him disrespecting me. I can handle it by myself."

He waved me off. "Too late for all that, they pulled guns on the team," He slid off the pool table then stared at all of us with contempt. "After I give y'all this work, sell it then go kill them niggaz. I'm not gon' re-up again until shit gets back under control." He walked out shaking his head.

We all sat there in silence not believing what we just heard. None of us were expecting to be cut off cause of some beef.

"This some bullshit nigga," Pusha spat.

"On gang," T-Rex spoke up.

It was a dozen niggaz with somber looks on their faces and I more than felt the pain. I knew once all the lil homies that weren't allowed at the meeting heard the news shit was gon' hit the fan. I shook my head feeling like it was mostly my fault.

"We gotta move real strategic now," Ray-Ray broke the silence. He was pacing with his hand under his chin deep in thought. "we can't focus on Juice and 'nem right now cause that's gon give the goonies the opportunity to blindside us. We gotta finish them off first then get at them other niggaz. It's perfect timing too cause since that day ain't nobody did nothing. Hopefully, they start lackin' thinking we ain't gon' retaliate."

"I'm with that." I agreed with him.

"Let's just hurry up and catch Flocko and Rico so the rest of them collapse. I'm bored with them weenies; I want Juice head on my fireplace." Flip rubbed his palms together with the look of death in his eyes.

"I'm getting Gunna," Pusha vowed, understandably.

"Yo J-money? You still falling back on yo baby mama?" Ray-Ray asked.

"I'm not fuckin wit that bitch right now cuz. The whole situation don't sit right with me." I got irritated just thinking about it.

"You gon' have to make up with her earlier than you expected to. She got the drop on all of them niggaz and we need 'em. Just play on her guilty conscience, women fall for that shit all the time. Make her prove her loyalty and I know she will. She knows she fucked up."

I wasn't feeling the shit for multiple reasons. First off, I wasn't ready to make up with her. I felt like whooping her ass every time she went through my mind. I also didn't wanna involve her in my street life. If the pigs ever snatched her up, I wanted her to be able to play dumb. A lot of shit can go wrong when using women especially if niggaz found out they were lining them up. But from the look I was getting from the team I knew I had to go with the program.

"I'll see what I can do, give me like a week to make her sweat." I gave in.

Ray-Ray shook me up. "It's important, we can't play with these niggaz blood."

I nodded in understanding.

"What we doing about JoJo and his niggaz?" JoJo asked

"They gotta get it too," T-Rex said, then looked right at me. "I know he damn near yo fam, but he violated in a major way. They gotta pay the fine for that, on gang."

I waved him off. "I don't give a fuck about that nigga; he chose his side. I'm putting a bullet through his head, on the set."

Chapter 18
Juice

I'd been back in the town for a few days now laying low like a muthafucka. I didn't wanna bust a move until we had everything, and everybody lined up to perfection. I already knew the streets were watching like crazy to see how the beef would play out. We definitely weren't gonna disappoint the fans, but I had too much money calling my phone. But I stayed stalking Lil Teflon and Dirty's social media to get their patterns down and info on their people. They were living it up, but I planned on being the reason for a while lot of tears and R.I.P. posts.

"A half a million? Niggaz ain't fuckin' with me!" I yelled to myself over the Young Dolph's music I had blasting through the speakers.

I was posted at my stash house all by myself counting my money. Ever since we came back from Seattle, I'd been sleeping over here not feeling like dealing with my naggin' ass baby mama. I was gon' sleep at a few bitches' houses that I fucked on the low but changed my mind. You never knew who was fuckin' on who in Portland, and I wasn't 'bout to give the opps an opportunity to catch me lackin'.

This shit crazy. I tuned off the money machines then leaned back on the couch with a big ass smile on my face. Life felt different when you were up, and I planned on seeing a milli real muthafuckin' soon. My phone went off snapping me outta my money zone.

My dick got hard when I saw It was Toya calling me. I knocked her a month ago and she had the craziest head game I'd ever had. Uncle Murda didn't lie when he said, *they suck it better when you rich!*

"What's poppin' baby?" I answered.

"You never told me if you was gon' slide through or not? I need some of that dick," she said in a sexy ass voice.

I looked at my watch, *a lil past eleven*. I really didn't feel like booking a hotel and her coming to me wasn't even an option. I hadn't had any pussy in a week so my lil' head was with it. I started debating whether or not I should trust her enough to pull up at her spot. She didn't have any red flags, but I remembered how Naughty and I did Marcel.

"I don't know baby. I'm posted right now." I tried to curve her.

"Listen to this." She replied, then got quiet for a few seconds.

I saw Twin calling me on the other line. Right when I was 'bout to click over, I started hearing a squishing sound. My meat got hard as a muthafucka! I declined his call fast.

"You hear that?" She moaned

"Yeah, baby. That muthafucka is wet as hell."

Maybe I can trust her.

Twin called back again. *Fuck this nigga want?*

I clicked over while she was moaning like crazy.

"I'm in the middle of something, what's good?" I answered.

"I got the drop on Flocko bitch ass!" Twin informed me.

I hopped off the couch instantly. I'd been searching for him ever since they shot me. I was gon' do that pussy real foul whenever I caught up with him.

"Coo, we gon' shit on it for a few days then crush his ass." I tried to keep my emotions in check.

"Naw shawdy, I mean I got the drop on the nigga right now. He's going to the afterlife in the next hour or so. This shit personal, I just figured you might want in on the action."

I closed my eyes and remembered the look of satisfaction on his face while they tried to gun me down. My temperature rose to the max.

"Where y'all at?"

"The caviar, I'm waiting in the lot."

"I'll be there in thirty." I hung up then clicked back over.

Toya was still making her pussy talk to me. *I can use her as an alibi.* I used that as an excuse to feed my dick.

"Yo Toya!"

"Yeah, daddy?" she moaned.

"I'll be there in an hour, gotta go."

I hung up then stood there with an evil grin. I couldn't believe the nigga had the heart to be at a strip club that everybody went to,

In the middle of a war. I didn't know if he wanted to earn a purple heart or what, but he was gon' have to rock that bitch in a casket.

I looked at the twin 4's on the table then shook my head. *Naw, he deserves better!* I went and grabbed the Draco from the closet. He thought he was a big dawg, so I was gon' hit 'em with the big shit. I wanted his funeral to be a closed casket, period. I put my vest on, then hopped in my scandalous ass Nissan that I'd copped for situations like this.

***

When I pulled up to the strip club, I was in full fledge 'G' mode, ready to eat the niggaz plate. The whole ride over, all I kept thinking about was how close he came to killing me. I kept picturing myself hiding under that car like a lil bitch.

"I'm here, where you at?" I asked Twin.

"You see the headlights blinking?"

I looked around the lot and spotted him. I pulled up right next to him then hopped in his Buick that I knew was stolen. He sat there looking like death itself. He had on all black from head to toe with a .40 Cal and a mask laying on his lap.

"So, what's the triv?" I asked.

"This bitch I fuck with works in here, she texted me that he was here. I told her to let me know when he's leaving," he told me.

"How deep are they?"

"She said it's just two of 'em. They in there trickin' while their homies been out here getting spanked."

"Who he in there with?"

"She ain't know." He shrugged his shoulders.

"It doesn't even matter. We crushin' the nigga too, whoever he is," I vowed.

"On the Mob," He agreed then looked me up and down "Where yo mask at, blood?"

"I ain't have one where I was at. I don't give a fuck anyways; I want my face to be the last one he ever sees. Plus, ain't no cameras out here, we good."

I leaned back and got comfortable for the wait. My mind went back to all the money I'd stacked up and what I planned on buying with it. I'd been grinding so hard that I didn't have the time to enjoy the shit. Every time I sold a brick all I could think about was selling another one. I'd been neglecting my family and putting my beef on the back burner for months. Muthafucka thought I changed but lil did they know how much. Talking to O-Dawg every day had really taken my mind to another level. Now I overstood the importance of money and war.

I was more than a street nigga now; I was a real gangsta. I had more responsibilities than I'd ever had and failing to meet them wasn't an option. My whole squad and their families depended on me to put the food on the plates. I had lawyer money stacked up for the inevitable cases that were sure to come. I was G'd up and more than ready to take shit to the next level.

"Yo, when that nigga freeze getting out?" Twin asked me about the human I hated the most.

His question threw me way the fuck off. My mind went from money back to murder in an instant.

"At the end of the year, why?"

"He the last nigga on O-Dawg kill list. Once he out the way all my debts are paid."

"Oh, you ain't gotta worry about that one. Ain't nobody killin that nigga but me, it's beyond personal." I laid down the law.

"I've been hearing a lil noise about some new rose city Crips. You heard anything?"

I looked at him like he was crazy. "Them niggaz are extinct and ain't never coming back. The ones we ain't get the chance to kill off ended up joining other gangs. Naw, I ain't heard no shit like that."

He nodded his head "I have. A few bitches told me some niggas been getting out the pun pushin that shit."

"Stop listening to these lying ass bitches," I snapped, losing my patience. "I run the town now if that shit was true I woulda been heard it. I don't give a fuck about none of that shit. The second he's released I'ma be in that lot waiting on him. He's not making it back to Portland, guaranteed." I punched the glove box letting my emotions get the best of me.

When it came to my big brotha I could never control my anger no matter how hard I tried. Seeing him killed in front of me ate at me for years. I'd lost count of how many nightmares I'd had since that night. I knew putting a bullet through his head was the only way to put a stop to them.

"Here they come." He read a text then put the phone in his pocket.

Good. I needed to take my anger out on somebody. I gripped the Draco with anger as my eyes scanned the lot for the enemy. I watched Twin slide the Obama mask over his head and had to respect his gangsta. The nigga stayed rubbing me the wrong way but when it was time to slide, he never ducked rec.

Another minute or two of waiting, then the suckaz came into view. I smiled when I saw who was next to Flocko with a bitch around his arm. *Rico.* Now I had both the niggaz that shot me right in my sight and I couldn't thank the game gods enough.

"Nigga, that's Rico too. We crushin' both of 'em and those bitches if they get in the way," I vowed.

"Say less."

I still couldn't believe they were only two deep, so I looked around for a car that could be packed with their shooters. I didn't see shit plus they were in Kobe range now and it was do-or-die time. We nodded at each other then bounced out.

"Murda Gang!"

"Mob!"

The bitches started screaming before we even fired a shot.

Yoppa! Yoppa! Yoppa! Boom! Boom! Boom! Flocko tried to reach but got ate up before he could pull it out. His eyes got wide in recognition right before he crumbled. Rico pushed his bitch in front of him for a shield then ran like a coward.

Yoppa! Yoppa! Boom! Boom! Boom!

We were on his ass tryna knock his head off. He reached behind and shot at us blindly like a real bitch. *Yoppa! Boom! Boom!* We tagged his back right when he thought he was getting away. He dropped in front of the main entrance and tried to get up and open it but fell back down. We speed-walked over to finish our meal.

The door opened and three security guards came out straight bustin! *Boom! Boom! Boc! Boc! Boc! Yoppa! Yoppa!* We shot back while backing up. The shit was getting outta control and I knew the real police would be on the way soon. They didn't follow us through the lot though they just stood their ground at the door. I guess they didn't want anybody actually running up in the club and shooting. We turned around and sprinted towards the whips.

"Help me!" Flocko was crying for help on his back.

He didn't know we were still on the scene or I'm sure he would have played dead. Either way, he was gon' die now. I stood right over his ho ass.

"Ain't no help in the jungle bitch. Tell the rest of those suckaz who sent you." I growled with hate.

"No!" He lifted his hands up.

Yoppa! Yoppa! One to the chest and the other one exploded his head. He'd be lucky to even have a closed casket.

I hopped in the whip and peeled out only half satisfied. I hoped that bitch ass Rico bled out and died.

Chapter 19
Juice

"Tell them suckaz, next time kill me." Gunna read Rico's post out loud.

He was mean mugging' the camera from the hospital bed, all wrapped up like a mummy. He had two young niggaz standing next to him showing their guns off.

We all started laughing at his fuck boy antics. We knew the truth about these niggaz.

"I heard you screamed like a bitch when them niggaz shot you. Rest in piss Flocko." Gunna read the comment out loud he's just posted.

Everybody laughed again. It was a few days after the murder and we were all posted up at Gunna's house, of course, the streets had a lot to say about Flocko getting spanked. That body really fucked those goonie niggaz up. Their reign was over and the whole town knows it, check mate. The funny thing was that a few of those Gas Team weenies were insinuating that they did it. Muthafuckaz in Portland stayed claiming bodies that they didn't have. I knew a few wars that got started like that. I shrugged the lies off, Rico knows who put them slugs in his back.

"I wish I was there so we could have killed those rent-a-cops and his bitch ass," Omar said.

"I still felt like we should go crush 'em for bustin' at y'all and saving that pussy's life," Mask added.

"On gang," Flash threw in.

"All that shit pointless, it is what it is. We need to focus on finishing the job. We should post at the hospital 'til he get out then spank them suckaz." TJ voiced what I'd been saying.

"Fuck that nigga, he a dead man walking. We gon' catch 'em slippin and purge his ho ass. I wouldn't be surprised if he had gang task walk 'em out. It's time to focus on knockin' them other suckaz off. I need to retaliate for my daughter, it's time," I told my niggaz.

"Oh, I almost forgot blood!" Mask jumped off the couch all excited. He punched his palm while speaking, he was charged up.

"Y'all remember the stripper bitch, Tweetie, I used to fuck on? I was on her IG the other day and found out that the lil sucka Dirty is her younger brother. I was all on that shit."

"You get back on her or what?" I asked.

"Nah, she got herpes. I'm boo on that," he answered.

I shook my head at his dumb ass. "You don't gotta actually fuck the bitch. Man, let me see what you talking about."

He pulled his phone out and showed us the comments and shit. We even saw a picture of them in the club posted on a couch. I recognized the bitch instantly then smiled when I thought of all the possibilities of how to use her to our advantage.

"Portland too small." I shook my head at the irony of the situation. She was gon' be the death of her brother and never even know it.

"It's always a bitch." Gunna spoke the truth that we were all thinking.

"Yo, can we hit the club up this weekend before we fuck it all off? Everybody been talking 'bout going, all the ho's gon' be there on my mama." Flash had the nerve to say.

"It *is* 'posed to be poppin though." TJ agreed.

I couldn't remember the last time I'd been to a club. *When O-Dawg was here.* I'd never been the clubbin' type of nigga. I was the one that used to wait in the lot then either rob the dope boyz or spank somebody that had money on their head. It was time to stunt on all the hating ass niggaz and take their bitches. Plus, I had some new jewels to show off. I smiled at the thought of the bitches faces while my diamonds hit the lights.

"Where it's at?" I asked.

Omar smiled then shook his head. "Dirty's the one downtown off of 5th and couch."

"Dirty's? Must be a sign, right? What you think brody?" I looked at Gunna.

He shrugged his shoulders. "Nigga let's go! We ain't hiding from shit and we ain't robbing no more, might as well."

"Can't nobody get no gun in; they don't play that shit," Flash informed.

"We don't need 'em, niggaz know what time it is with us." I let my arrogance get the best of me.

Chapter 20
Jamar

"We should have been left her ass cuz, she taking way too long. I don't know why bitches always taking forever." I complained to Pusha about Naughty.

"You can't leave yo wifey, big bro. Here." He passed me the Backwood.

I let the weed calm my nerves for a few seconds. I'd been on edge more than ever since Flocko got his stupid ass crushed. A lot of people thought we did it, but we didn't. So only those Murda Gang niggaz could be responsible, In my eyes. We had to be on point from them and any of the few remaining goonies. The crazy thing is we still hadn't bumped heads with Juice or nobody from his hood. Not a word, a threat, nothing.

I took Ray-Ray's advice and came back home to Naughty. I wasn't about to fuck my family up over his bitch ass. I trusted my bitch, but I was still making her prove her loyalty. If she wanted me in her life, then she was gon' have to drop the info on juice. So far, she'd given me some locations on where they posted up at. The only thing she wouldn't spit out was his mother's address. Talking about she got love for the bitch! But it was only a matter of time.

"Naughty! Hurry up! Niggaz waiting on us!" I yelled at her again.

"Here I come, shit!" She yelled back.

She stepped into the front room looking like a video vixen. She spun around real slow giving me a show. She had on a lil' ass red dress, high heels, and had her hair flowing down her back. She looked perfect. *Damn!*

"You like?" She asked with a big ass smile on her face.

I pulled her in and palmed her ass. "I love."

We kissed a few times then I pulled her ass to the car. It took us twenty minutes to get to the club Dirty's that was downtown. I fuckin' hated going downtown, but it's where all the poppin functions were always held. Tonight was no exception either. Dirty's was already one of the hottest clubs in the town but tonight It was the only hot spot. They were throwing an end-of-the-summer party and women got in free all night. Everybody was on the net claiming they were pulling up. Most of them niggaz were just cappin' though, they didn't have enough diamonds to be in the presence of money.

"Yo ray-ray said pull up all the way in the back," Pusha said then hung up.

The homies were deep as a muthafucka when I pulled up. It was at least thirty niggaz standing against their cars with their bitches or was tryna knock one walking by. We had it lookin like a music video out this bitch! I hopped out the Benz turnt up to the max. All my niggaz were here, I was feeling myself.

"Gas gang!" I yelled and threw up the set for the homies.

"Gas!" Everybody yelled back.

I made my way through the crowd shaking up the whole team.

"Oh shit! It's real now!" I got pumped up seeing D-roc leaning on his blue Lamborghini with some bad yellow chick.

He hadn't been out with us since I'd been out the pen, so I was surprised to see him.

We shook up. "Yeah, I had to make a cameo real quick. Let these niggaz see who really getting money and we ain't hiding from shit," he replied.

"Cuz let's go inside now so we can buy V.I.P out and knock some bitches." Flip walked up.

"C'mon, we out," D-Roc said.

We mobbed to the front of the line daring somebody to say something, got patted down then walked in. It was all eyes on us as we floated to V.I.P. but that's exactly what we expected. I wrapped my arm around Naughty while my eyes scanned for any of our enemies. It was so muthafuckin' packed it was hard to spot everybody, but I damn sho' tried. My squad was deep so that gave me comfort in the worst-case scenario, fighting.

"What's up wit it?" Breeze said as we walked by their V.I.P. section. He had faith sitting on his lap.

"Shit, 'bout to stunt. Y'all ready to keep up?" I shook him up then nodded at his hit squad homies.

They were coo' but I knew Juice's big brother was from their hood when he got spanked. So, I didn't know how they would feel after we killed his bitch ass. I didn't feel any tension from them though at that moment.

"We doubling whatever y'all do, off top." He shot back with a cocky smile on his face.

After Naughty and faith hugged, we walked off to our section. Some young niggaz that went by the Murk unit were in the section right next to ours. I knew who they were because some of my lil' niggaz fucked with a few of 'em. I also knew they had funk with JoJo and his homies. I wasn't with having the enemy of my enemy as my friend shit. If you weren't gang, then you wasn't shit to me, period.

"Sup cuz?" I nodded at them outta respect.

"What's good?" Their leader Teflon responded to me.

We posted up and made the waitress work hard for her money. We ordered everything they had to offer in that bitch. I looked at Naughty and noticed the sour look on her face.

"What's wrong baby?"

"He's the one that be getting into it with my brother." She looked at Teflon then rolled her eyes.

"Don't worry about that shit. Yo brother killed his manz, not the other way around. Let's be happy and enjoy the night baby. We'll deal with the bullshit another day," I kissed her then handed her a bottle. "Drink with yo nigga."

"Not right now daddy, I'm waiting on Jessie." She kissed me with a smile on her face now.

She gon' be sick when we spank her brother.

I wish I could spare her the pain of JoJo's funeral, but I knew I couldn't. The damage was done. All I could do was console her at the time and lie to her that some other niggaz did it.

"Gas team! Gas team!" Ray-ray yelled with a bottle of rose in his hand.

"Gas!" we all yelled back.

Within seconds we were standing on couches and throwing up gang signs to Future's newest song. We were doing what we did best, stunt on niggaz. We were the talk of the town and wasn't nothing nobody could do about it. If muthafuckaz in the club felt some type of way, they knew to keep the shit to themselves. We wasn't worried about nothing.

Chapter 21
Naughty

I sat there watching my baby daddy and his homies turning up like they ruled the world. I was glad that he came back home and decided to work things out with me. But the secret I was keeping from him would eventually destroy our relationship. I was almost a month pregnant and one hundred percent sure it was by Juice. When I found out days ago, I was devastated beyond words. I tried hard as I could to make it Jamar's, but it wasn't. I'd just gotten off my period the day before I fucked Juice and I still hadn't fucked Jamar. He would only let me suck his dick since he came back home. That was his way of punishing me. I was so confused about what to do that I barely slept at night. Faith kept telling me to act like it was Jamar's and Jessie wanted me to get an abortion. I was firmly against baby killing and I couldn't do Jamar like that. Whatever choice I made I knew would shatter my world. Especially since I made the decision to give me and Jamar a real chance. He deserved it and my son deserved to have his real father in the house with him.

I'm here. Come to the bathroom! Right now! I read the text from Jessie then hopped up. I just knew she had some bad news to tell me.

"Jessie just got here, I'm gonna meet her at the bathroom," I told Jamar over the loud ass music.

"Come right back, don't make me come to snatch you up. If she wanna be all up in niggaz faces, that's on her but you won't be a part of it," he threatened.

"I know daddy." I gave him a kiss then made my way to the bathroom.

I had to make my way through multiple crowds of perverts and broke niggaz tryna holla at me that was too scared to try it in front of Jamar. They were lucky I was in a rush and didn't feel like causing a scene. Soon as I got by the bathroom, I recognized somebody that made my stomach drop. *Gunna!* I could spot his evil ass from a mile away. I already knew if he was here, then Juice couldn't be too far away. It was a group of them niggaz, but I hurried up and got into the bathroom before any of them spotted me.

"Bitch is that Gunna?!" I panicked.

She nodded. "Hell yeah! And Juice is here with all his niggaz and so is your brother. I t ain't looking good, Miami." She looked more scared than me.

"Did they see you? What they say?"

"Juice was like, I know Naughty here with you tell her she leaving with me." She made her voice deep.

Aww, shit! "What? Do they know Jamar and them are here?"

"Naw," She shook her head "They were all smiles and shit but it's only a matter of time before they run into each other."

"Fuck!" I stomped my feet in frustration. "Them niggaz don't ever go out and the one time they do just gotta be tonight!"

"So, what you gon' do? You tell him you're pregnant?"

I screwed my face up. "Hell no! and I'ma go sit back down next to my baby daddy before he comes looking for me and sees Juice."

"I'm going with faith, fuck that shit. I ain't tryna be in the middle of no gang fights and I really don't need Juice wanting to kill me." She sounded scared as hell.

I was irritated she was leaving me by myself, but I understood where she was coming from. Once Juice felt like you weren't on his side then you were dead to him that moment. You probably would end up dead in real life. I couldn't believe I was pregnant by his psychotic ass.

Chapter 22
Juice

"Tell my bitch she's leaving with me," I told Jessie.

"Uhh, okay Juice. I'll tell her." She looked scared then walked off a lil too quickly.

She must still be spooked from the last situation.

The Club was poppin' like a muthafucka by the time we made our grand entrance. We mobbed in that bitch twenty deep daring a nigga to say something. We were the bad guys that nobody wanted to see at the top of the food chain but there wasn't nothing they could do about it, we were here. I recognized a few niggaz that we'd stripped for their Jewelry back in the day. Either they slightly nodded at us or they turned their heads like they didn't see us. Long as they kept shit copasetic then we would keep their lil secrets.

The bitches were jocking us hard as a muthafucka like we were athletes or some shit. Bitches had a sixth sense for real niggaz with money. We snatched a few of 'em up and had them roll to V.I.P with us. I saw a few random niggaz eye Pistol Pete's ex medallion that hung from my neck. I didn't give two fucks though; I came to make a statement. I was heavy on the ice too! I had all three of my chains on, plus my rollie and my pinky ring on. I was daring somebody to touch them real nigga diamonds.

"I don't see no opps in this muthafucka blood!" Gunna yelled over the music.

I kept scanning the room and was lowkey surprised he was right.

"They know better,
gang," I responded

The waitress led us to a V.I.P section that was connected to the section that the Hit Squad had rented out. I was good with that.

"What's brackin' big bro?" Gunna shook Breeze up excited to see him.

"What's poppin nigga? I thought y'all didn't like to party?"

Gunna shrugged his shoulders. "Things done changed."

"Okay, I see y'all," Breeze nodded along then stuck his hand out to me. "What's good Lil Juice?"

I noticed faith sitting on his lap looking like the gold digger that she was. She waved at me with a phony ass smile on her face. *I know Naughty ain't here with them!* She was gon' make me drag her ass up outta there by her hair.

"What's hood with you? I see y'all in here turning up to the max." I responded.

"Yeah, we doing our thang, but you," He grabbed Pistol Pete's ex chain. "Are really doing yo thang. Don't go too hard though lil bruh. The moment they start to fear you is when they gon' try to really kill you. And if that doesn't work, they'll put the pigs on you." He dropped a Jewel on me that I didn't care for.

"I hear you, but the damage is already done. All the niggaz that disrespected us on our rise to the top gotta get it. I'm not looking to make new enemies but my old ones gotta die, period." I kept it raw.

"Well, either way, I know yo brother is proud of the way you're moving. Keep getting yo money blood."

We shook up again then I turned my focus on Faith. "I have already seen Jessie, so what's up with Naughty? Where she at?" I looked around to make sure she wasn't entertaining no hit squad niggaz. She knew how I really felt about them.

"I don't know," She shot back then shrugged her shoulders. "She's grown and I'm not a babysitter."

I screwed my face up instantly. She was tryna flex and have a smart mouth because she was sitting on Breezy's lap. She must have forgotten how I got down.

"Yo, all that extra attitude gon' get you hurt in here. I don't give a fuck who's dick you riding on, I don't tolerate disrespect and you know that. You know me, so don't play," I spat while staring dead in her eyes.

She looked at Breeze for help. I didn't give two fucks how he felt about the bitch. If he wanted to die over a gold digger that was his business. I didn't like them niggaz like that anyways. I was looking for a reason.

"She over there with them Gas Team niggaz, blood," Jimmy pointed towards the end of the club. "She in here with Jamar."

Faith had a lil smirk on her face that I was debating on slappin' off her face.

"C'mon blood, let's order some bottles. Fuck that bitch and those niggaz." Omar whispered in my ear.

I nodded then stared at faith with hate. *That's gon' cost you.*

We posted up on the couches then sent the waitress on a field trip.

I stared to the back of the club and saw a bunch of niggaz standing on couches with bottles in their hands. I knew it was the suckaz. I wasn't worried about those pussies not one bit, but I felt a way about my bitch being in their presence. I could care less if she had a baby with the sucka or not. If shit was that deep, she wouldn't have still been fuckin' on me and texting me. It was the principalities of the situation. Her being with those lames was a spit in me and my niggaz faces.

"Yo sister really playing with my patience and my gangsta." I leaned over and spoke low to JoJo.

"Shit will play out in our favor, don't trip," he said, then went back to whispering in some chick's ear.

Ten minutes later I was sipping on some Cîroc getting madder by the minute. I was the only one that wasn't smiling with a bitch in my face. I looked up and saw Gunna staring at me.

"What's up nigga?" I growled. I didn't feel like hearing his mouth about Naughty.

"Fuck Gas Team nigga!" He screamed out to my surprise.

"Fuck Gas Team!" I shot back.

Everybody got dead quiet. I recognized what Gunna was doing for me. He knew how bad I wanted to push up on them suckaz. I couldn't be the one to set it off cause then everybody would say I was trippin' over a bitch. But if Gunna popped it off that would be expected. He stood on the couch and turnt up.

"Blood, fuck Gas Team! And fuck this club! I'm not sitting here while the opps are in here! Woop!"

Once muthafuckaz started ‘wooping’ back I knew it was on. Nobody could rile a bunch of wolves up like Gunna, period. He jumped off the couch and strolled like Tupac did in Vegas, straight to their section. I was right next to him ready for whatever. I know everybody that saw us mobbin’ already knew what time it was. We had muthafuckaz parting like the red sea, it was crazy.

Them gas team niggaz saw us coming and stood up waiting on us like they were really about that life. I saw Naughty sitting on the couch looking good as a muthafucka in a red dress. When we locked eyes, she put her head down. She knew she’d betrayed me. Jamar and Flip stood by each other with their arms folded like they were Suge Knight or some shit.

Right when we were closing in on them, some young niggaz stood up in the section before theirs. After I made eye contact with a few of them I forgot all about Jamar’s bitch ass. These suckaz were at the very top of my kill on sight list. I looked at Gunna, JoJo, and Omar to make sure they were seeing what I was. They nodded at me. It was on.

“Aye nigga, yo name Teflon, right?” I walked right up on him.

He shrugged his shoulders. “Ask that ho ass nigga right there.” He nodded at JoJo.

“Yo manz right here shot at me with my daughter, you about that?” I pointed at Lil Teflon and Dirty.

He smiled at me. “You said that to say what?”

Whap!

I hit Lil Teflon in his head with a bottle dropping his ass. Gunna snuffed Teflon then it was on! We all rushed each other like gladiators.

Chapter 23
Jamar

"Yo manz right here shot at me with my daughter."

Once Juice said that I knew it was on. Damn, I never knew it was the Murk Unit niggaz that tried to end his life. I wish they would have got his ass. Me and my niggaz were more than ready to rumble with those lames but I guess they wanted an easier fight. Both crews were fuckin' it up but Juice and 'em were getting the better of the Murk units. Me and Flip locked eyes and it was on. We couldn't let them niggaz get away with that stunt at my shop. I grabbed a bottle then charged with a vengeance.

Whap!

I hit one of those pussies with the bottle then locked my sights on Juice. He was low-key working Teflon. "What's crackin cuz!" I yelled then hit Juice with a two-piece.

He stumbled backwards then threw his hands up like he was ready. Soon as he recognized who it was, he went for his waist. Nothing. I smiled.

"Ain't no guns in here to save yo bitch ass now nigga!" I taunted while closing the distance.

I saw it in his eyes that he was scared to fight, it didn't' matter though, the check had been cashed.

"You a bitch nigga!" he yelled then threw a wild ass haymaker.

I slipped it with ease then waved him forward so he could try again. Everybody around me was fighting and yelling but I was zoned in on my man. I used to dream about beating him to death when I was locked up. I rushed forward and put the paws on him with ease. His hand game was pure garbage. He got one good hit in then he was against the wall getting drilled.

"Talk that shit now!" I gave him hella body blows that brought all the bitch outta him.

The next thing I knew, two young niggaz from Teflon's crew started punching on him too. We were working him! The one I knew as Dirty snatched his chain off his neck while still punching him.

"Give me the homies chain bitch!" Dirty yelled.

Then something crashed against my head making me see stars for a second. I turned around and saw Omar squaring up with me. I touched my head and felt all the blood pouring from it. Right when I put my hands up to give the fat nigga this work all the lights came on inside the club. I looked around and saw everybody still fighting, it was going down.

"The cops are on the way!" The promoter yelled through a bull-horn.

Then hella security guards rushed in like they were real S.W.A.T. or something. They started grabbing a few niggaz up. Omar and I smiled at each other knowing we'd see each other again.

"I'm telling y'all right now cuz, whoever put their hands on me I'm killin yo mother. Y'all know how me and my niggaz rock," I threatened security after they rushed me and Omar.

They froze in their tracks. They knew I wasn't bluffing about this crippin' at all. I turned my back on them and ran to grab my bitch who was on the couch looking petrified. I snatched her up then scrambled like everybody else up out that muthafucka. I stayed on point the whole time though cause niggaz like to snuff their opps when it was crowded. I stayed close as I could to my homies while we tried to weave through all the bullshit. We had way too many guns in our cars to be playing around with. Fuck that!

Chapter 24
Juice

My eye was shut, and I could barely see out of the other one, but my demons were directing me. My brotha's chain was missing and I've never felt more hatred in my life! *Give me the homies chain!* The words kept playing over and over in my head and I knew exactly who said it.

"Juice c'mon nigga the boys are here!" Twin yelled at me after I grabbed the Mac-10 from under the seat.

I didn't give a fuck about none of that shit! The suckaz had my chain and somebody had to die behind that. I walked right past my niggaz on my solo shit. I saw all the cop cars, but I also saw groups of niggaz still leaving the club and jogging to their cars. I just had to catch one of my enemies.

"Juice, fall back nigga." T.J. grabbed me by the arm.

I spun around quickly with the Mac pointed right at his face. I was tired of the nigga questioning my actions and now he was tryna stop me from retaliating about my brotha. He looked surprised but for some reason, he didn't have a drop of fear in his eyes. I couldn't decide if he just wasn't scared to die or if he didn't believe I would push his shit back.

"What you saying nigga? Those niggaz got my dead brotha's chain and you scared to ride!?" I screamed in his face.

The liquor in my system had my anger intensified to the max. I was more than ready to treat him like the opposition if he said the wrong words.

"So, we pulling guns on each other now? That's what we're doing?" I'ma chop it up to the liquor plus yo emotions right now." He slowly pushed the heat out of his face then walked away.

I looked at my niggaz and Gunna shook his head no. He knew I was debating on shooting him in the back. JoJo grabbed his heat out of the trunk then walked up.

"I'm with you bruh."

His words touched my heart. He knew I was on a suicide mission and still he was gon' rock out. I was surprised he was the most loyal in my time of need. I nodded at him then spun around back on my trip. I gave no fucks about all the pigs in the lot. I came to get my manz, period. I spotted them Murk Unit bitches speed walking to their whips. They were tryna put distance between them and the boys, but I was the one they should have feared.

I kept my eyes on them and the pigs while we crouched low between parked cars. I wanted to get close but not too close where I couldn't get away. The pigs really weren't focused on them. They were focusing on escorting crowds out of the club. *Fuck it!* I looked at JoJo then popped up.

Boom! Boom! Boom! Boom! Boc! Boc! Boc!

We let those suckaz have it right in front of the law. Everybody started running through the lot for their lives making it hard for the boys to pinpoint our location. I saw somebody from their circle drop down to his knees. I zoomed in on Teflon's head and squeezed the trigga while he ran. I wanted to drop the leader and get the rest later.

Boom! Boom! Boc! Boc! Boc! Boom! Boom! Boom!

We put the flame back on 'em until the pigs started bustin' on us.

"C'mon nigga we out!" I told JoJo then sprinted to the whip.

Boom! Boom! Boom!

I heard the shots coming from behind me, so I busted back without looking or aiming. My heart was pounding out of my chest. I saw all our niggaz running to their whips now and peeling out. I hopped in the Bentley and mashed out as soon as JoJo jumped in. I don't think I took one breath from the moment I first shot until I left the lot. I wasn't even kinda satisfied though. Nobody left the earth and them fuck niggaz still had my brotha's chain!

Chapter 25
Juice

Sniff! Sniff!

I sniffed a mountain of cocaine through my nose then leaned back on the couch high as a kite. I didn't know what time it was, but I knew it was early in the morning and I hadn't had a minute of sleep yet. I had the Draco on my lap and my vest on my chest with the news on mute. We hit some nigga named Paul in the leg that ran with the other side. *Fuck 'em.*

I'd been getting high for hours and fantasizing about killing all my enemies. All of them. I was gon' start with the Murk Unit for snatching my chain. They had no idea how bad they'd just fucked up. They were dancing with the devil now and I was gon' snatch every single one of their souls. I wasn't gon' show them any mercy. I wasn't gonna knock the main niggaz off then let the rest scatter. Naw! They all were gonna get it.

Them pussies were just desert though, something sweet to ear until we got to the real meal. I was licking my chops just thinking about Jamar. He was pretty nice with his hands, I couldn't front. That UFC shit only mattered in the pen and I couldn't wait to show him how deadly I was with my hands gripping a pistol.

"Fuck these niggaz want!?" I shouted at my phone that was ringing for the hundredth time.

I'd blocked every nigga from my squad that called my phone. I felt like these niggaz pulled their skirts up when I needed them to move with me. That shit ain't sit right with me. Plus, they kept texting me about the triv with TJ, which was unimportant to me.

I saw the number wasn't saved in my contacts and decided to answer.

"Who the fuck is this?"

"This big Teflon," he said like I should have known his voice.

"So dead men can talk, it's a miracle. Yo days are numbered you bitch ass nigga," I spat.

"Check the pic I just sent to you."

I looked at the screen and saw I had a new pic. I opened it and saw my brotha's chain laying on a table. I prayed to Satan I could jump through the phone and take his life. I opened my eyes and got upset I was still on my couch.

"My lil nigga didn't mean to grab this chain he went for Pete's chain." He explained what I already knew.

"You said that to say what?"

"I'll give you back yo brotha's chain in exchange for Pete's. You've worn it long enough disrespecting him."

I gave his proposal some thought then hit another line of powder. I did want my chain back but at what cost? I pictured what my brotha would say and how he would roll in his grave if I went out like a bitch! He told me if I ever got it took from me not to talk to him until I killed the man responsible.

"Nigga, fuck you and bitch-ass Pete!" I jumped off the couch slapping my vest. "I'ma kill you then snatch it off yo neck, pussy! I'm killin kids and everything about that chain so if you smart you better leave that muthafucka somewhere then run! I'm comin' for you!" I yelled then hung up.

I tossed the phone then started pacing, mad as a muthafucka.

"Nigga gon' call my phone playing let's make a deal! I don't know who the fuck he thinks I am!" I yelled at myself.

"Davontae, why the hell are you in here yelling? And it's early in the morning." Brittney rushed in with an attitude, fixing her robe.

I looked her up and down then waved her off. "Take yo ass back to sleep." I went back to pacing like she wasn't there.

"I can't!" she raised her voice like she was crazy.

"You're in here screaming all morning. Is this coke?" She bent over the table then mugged me. "Are you out of your fuckin mind? You're doing cocaine out here while your daughter is in her room? What if she comes out here? What's wrong with you? You need to get yo shit together. Out here with guns and dope and shit!"

"Whatever bitch, I don't hear you complaining when You're spending that drug money." I shot back then went back to pacing.

"Ugg! Fuck you!" She knocked the powder to the ground thinking that would make me mad.

I shrugged my shoulders. "I got kilos of that shit." I laughed at her childish ass. She complained that I was being too loud but came in yelling louder than me. I didn't have the time to be arguing with her, so I kept walking around ignoring her ass. My mind was on killing dirty.

"I lost my brotha's chain, just go back to sleep and leave me alone," I told her after she kept talking and talking.

"I don't give a fuck about that chain you need to- "

My hand was around her neck before she could finish her blasphemous statement. I slammed her on the couch while tightening my grip. Now my anger was focused on her. She started clawing at my hands, but it was pointless.

"Bitch don't ever disrespect my brotha! You hear me!?" I yelled in her face.

She nodded. I let her go and watched her gasp for air. She was lucky I didn't kill her dumb ass. I didn't know what the fuck had gotten into her, but it would get her ass whooped if she didn't get it right.

"I got jumped and niggaz took Juice chain then I gotta come home and beef with you?" I growled at her.

She still couldn't talk. My phone started going off again. I answered it when I saw it was JoJo.

"What's good?"

"Them suckaz on Snapchat with yo chain, blood."

"They just called me like twenty minutes ago! I'ma pull up on you in thirty." I hung up then went to Snapchat.

I hurried up and clicked on the video. The first thing I saw was dirty rockin' my chain! The hate instantly consumed me.

Then about ten niggaz I recognized from the club started speaking ill on my gangsta. They ended the video by saying fuck Murda Gang, fuck my brotha's grave and claimed they would sell the chain to anybody for ten bands.

I replayed it then shoved it in Brittney's face so she could understand my anger. I didn't' even give her time to speak to me. I grabbed my shit then left the house.

***

"Damn blood, so the nigga tried to swap you chains? That nigga done got bold suddenly." JoJo said then passed me the Backwood.

I'd just got done giving him the play-by-play about the call I had with Teflon. We were posted in his living room planning a bunch of suckaz funerals.

"Yeah, it's easy to be a brave heart over the phone and a computer. He wasn't talking though when I was beating his ass last night." I shot back.

"Facts," he paused, then looked at me funny like he had something on his mind. "What's the triv with TJ? That shit was brazy."

I shrugged my shoulders. "I don't know and don't care right now. If he ain't riding, then fuck 'em."

"You better watch that nigga, something is off with ol' boy."

I nodded but not really giving a fuck. TJ knew better than to cross the gang.

"You got a drop on one of them suckaz or what? I ain't bring this Draco out for no reason."

"I heard a few of them niggaz be in some apartments off 162nd posted outside."

"You down for a field trip?" He smirked at me.

"That can't be a real question."

***

"On my mama, nigga, I'm hoppin out and hitting whoever out here that even looks like they fuck with Murk Unit. Anybody with dreads, sagging or anything similar," I vowed when we pulled up ten minutes later.

It was broad day and we ain't have on no masks or none of that shit. We were on some hot boy shit fo'real about my dead brotha. I wanted the whole town to know who did it.

"You wanna pull in first to scope it out or just park and get on foot?" JoJo asked.

"Pull in first. Ain't no point in having the pigs getting called if we ain't gon' kill nobody."

"Yup," he replied, then slowly entered the lot.

"Have you talked to yo' sister?" I asked out of nowhere.

"We texted early this morning. Sis on some other shit I ain't gon' lie. She talking about, she can't split her family up just 'cause we can't get along with Jamar."

His words cut right through my heart. I thought she was my bitch forever and here she was turning her back on me when I needed her the most. *Bitches ain't shit!*

"You know where they stay?"

He shook his head. "Naw I never been there, and I know she ain't gon' tell me now. Don't trip, we gon' knock him off then she all yours."

I nodded then started focusing on my surroundings. I didn't spot anybody that looked like they were with this gang shit. Just mostly lil kids out playing.

"I think we got one blood," JoJo spoke low.

"Where?" I looked around not seeing shit.

"See that nigga sitting on the car right there?"

He pointed down the lot. "I can't say fo'sure but that looks like Moe's bitch-ass."

"He on their roster?"

"He was there last night," he gave me a look then kept driving. I'ma drive past 'em to make sure it's him. If it is, we gon' park around the corner then bounce out."

I acted like I was on my phone as we rode up on him. Soon as we got close enough, I instantly recognized him. Moe was sitting on a car talking on a phone with a big ass grin on his face. Must *be some fresh pussy.* We were gonna knock that smile right off his face. We made eye contact for a split second as we passed, and I had a feeling he spotted us I turned my head real quick tryna play it off. *Fuck!*

"I think he saw us brody," I told JoJo.

He stopped right on the spot. "Shit. Fo'real?"

"Yeah, we locked eyes."

"Fuck it, let's find out." He jumped out with his heat in his hand.

I followed suit without a second thought. When we turned the corner, we saw him walking fast as a muthafucka while on his phone. We started speed walking after him.

We were tryna get close as possible before he saw us. I wanted to get right up on him, make the shit personal. He turned his head and spotter us on his ass. He stuffed his phone in his pocket then took off full speed.

Yoppa! Yoppa! Yoppa! Boom! Boom!

We started letting that hot shit fly while we chased after him. I was tryna knock his chest out with the Draco. All I needed was for one bullet to connect and that was gon' be his ass. But he was fast as fuck putting mad distance between us.

Yoppa! Yoppa! Boom! Boom! Boom!

Usain bolt couldn't outrun a bullet so I knew this pussy couldn't. We stayed on his ass. He ran up some stairs tryna get inside an apartment. We kept bustin'. He got low as the shells were connecting with the rail and stairs. He had to either be the luckiest Muthafucka alive or had an angel protecting him.

Yoppa! Yoppa!

He made it inside against all odds.

"Fuck!" I screamed out, then climbed halfway up the stairs.

Boom! Boom! Boom! Yoppa! Yoppa! Yoppa! Yoppa!

We chopped that muthafucka down! We had slugs flying through the door and the window with hopes of knocking his head off.

"C'mon nigga!" JoJo yelled then took off to the whip.

I broke after him mad as fuck. I should have bounced out as soon as we locked eyes. I knew better.

Chapter 26
Juice

The last week has been hectic as a muthafucka in the streets but I could care less. After our failed attempt on Moe's life, they decided to let their nuts hang and come holla at us. They caught Flash coming out of the liquor store and ended up poppin' him in the thigh. He brushed that baby shit off and rode the same night.

The news was still covering the shooting from the club only because we tried to hit the cops. My name was on fire about that shit, but my lawyer said I didn't have a warrant so fuck it. Mask bumped heads with Pusha, and they clacked it out, but nobody got hit. So now it was officially on with them faggots too, but I still didn't give a fuck.

"Look, ain't nobody tryna push you out, my nigga. We just feel like you way too hot and got a death wish to focus on the business side right now. Nigga, you just shot at the pigs." Jaxx tried to reason with me.

We'd been at the stash spot for over twenty minutes discussing the same shit but not getting nowhere. I knew from the moment he called and told me to meet him and Twin, it was gon' be some funny shit.

"I don't give a fuck about none of that, I'll never let another nigga feed my team, not for a single day. No disrespect Twin, but you ain't even gang. You're mob life and we're Murda Gang, Period."

"I've been riding with you like I'm Murda Gang though," Twin shot back.

I shrugged my shoulders. "That's yo choice. But you've also been rockin' with those Inglewood Family niggaz tough too."

"You do realize that we're having this talk out of respect for you and what you did? I don't need your permission to supply my lil' nigga with my dope." Jaxx was getting frustrated.

"I understand that fully, but you're not gon' supply him and have him take my place at my own table. Now, if he wanna go eat with them Inglewood niggaz that's his business. But I don't think my squad will like him selling the same work with some other niggaz, especially if he lowers the price." I stared Twin right in the eyes, hoping he understood my threat. He smiled at me.

My phone started ringing. I saw it was Latoya for the fifth time and I got worried something was wrong with my daughter.

"Yo, what's the problem? I'm busy right now," I answered this time.

"Rocky got something important for you. Come over here today. I wanna see you ASAP," she spoke.

Her words threw me off like a muthafucka.

"Aight, I'm on the way." I hung up.

I got off the couch done with the pointless conversation with them two niggaz. I had shit to do.

"I gotta go check on something real quick. In the meantime, I'ma keep slanging the work and exterminating my enemies."

"I'll holla at O-Dawg and let you know," Jaxx replied.

"You do that," I said then walked out.

***

"I'm pulling up right now," I told Latoya then hung up.

The whole thirty-minute drive my mind kept racing and wondering what the fuck did rocky want. We didn't rock like that, so it had to be really important for him to reach out to me. *Better not be no dope or money.* I hopped out with my hand close to my waist just in case shit went sour. I didn't believe Latoya would help set me up but a gun to head or loved one could make muthafuckaz change up quickly. My paranoia was through the roof.

"What's good bro?" Rocky opened the door and stuck his hand out.

I looked past him and saw Latoya sitting on the couch with a smile on her face. I let my guard down.

"Shit, tryna survive, what's hood?" I shook him up then walked inside.

I gave baby mama a hug then sat down. Rocky started pacing while rubbing his palms together. I knew he had something heavy to lay on me. I looked at Latoya with a skeptical look and she gave me a nod of approval.

"Somebody gon' tell me why I'm here or what?" I was tired of waiting.

He stopped pacing now. "We've been seeing all the bullshit over the net and we ain't feeling how they got yo' brother's chain."

"I'm still confused on how you let them take it," Latoya snapped. I mugged her hard. "I mean, I know how much it means to you. I loved your brother too." She tried to clean it up.

"The bitch nigga snatched it while we were all fighting in the club. It was a real ho' move. You know I'd rather swallow a bullet than to give that muthafucka up," I spat.

"I know where Lil Teflon lay his head at," Rocky blurted out.

I screwed my face up. I was confused on how the fuck a nobody like him could find out something that me and my niggaz couldn't.

"Oh yeah?" I kept my composure

"Yeah," he nodded. "I was at my other baby mama spot yesterday and saw him across the street. He was at this bitch named Kim's house all day."

"How you know it's him? You see him?"

"Naw, but he the only nigga in Portland with a gold Charger. After I saw it parked in her driveway, I asked my BM about it and her messy ass gave me the whole run down. That's his main bitch and he's always over there, according to her."

I nodded along with the story. It sounded like a typical fuck up that niggaz stayed making. Fuckin' with a bitch that everybody knew or that stayed in the hood. Somebody was gon' always see you, it never failed. Then the dummy had the audacity to park a one-of-a-kind car in the driveway? He wasn't used to beefing with real wolves, but he was gon' learn the hard way.

"Where the spot at?" I asked.

"Over there by Woodlawn park, on 6th and Morgan."

I shook my head at the young niggaz deadly mistake.

My phone went off snapping me out of my visualization of killing him in his gold Charger. I saw it was Gunna.

"I just got the drop on Lil Teflon, suit up gang," I answered, ready to make my move.

"We gon' need it blood." He growled

"What happened?" I knew something was wrong. I exhaled getting ready for the bad news.

"Jamar just bought yo chain for ten thou from dirty. It's all over the gram. They being disrespectful, it's bad."

I gripped the phone in anger. My whole body heated up. *Stay Clam* "On my brotha grave we killin' that nigga! Tell everybody to meet at JoJo spot right now!" I yelled then hung up.

I looked at Latoya and Rocky with the look of the devil then got on Instagram. We watched the video together in disbelief. Jamar handed the money over then Dirty put it around his neck like he was fuckin' King Tut. Jamar had the biggest smirk on his face then stared at the chain.

"I'ma send yo lil brotha to come live with yo bitch ass. Gas team, fuck Murda Gang and the goonies."

The net was going crazy! The video and picture had over a thousand likes and comments and it had only been up for half an hour. I'd never been disrespected like this.

"What you want for the info?" I asked Rocky.

He shook his head. "You put me on my feet, I owe that to you." He shook my hand.

That was the moment I knew I'd made the right decision to squash our beef. Cause if I hadn't, he would have been selling me out to my enemies and I would have never saw it coming. That was one time I was glad I'd pushed my pride to the side.

"I was gon' go talk to Lisa before I left but now, I don't think I should. I don't want this evil shit to rub off on her. Plus, I don't know when the next time I'ma be back over here. I gotta focus on killin' these niggaz," I said then shook my head at their level of disrespect.

"I disagree with you," Latoya stood up with her hands on her hips. "I think you need to go back there and see your daughter, so you remember what you're fighting for. You're more valuable than a chain to her. A chain can be replaced, you can't." She lectured.

I nodded. I felt where she was coming from but spending time with my daughters always made me feel soft and I needed to stay in goon mode. I tried to explain this to her, but she wasn't going for it.

"Lisa! Your daddy here to see you!" She yelled out.

I stared her up and down mad as shit.

"Daddy?! Hi daddy!" She saw me then went crazy. She ran to me then I had to push my 'G' to the side.

Chapter 27
Naughty

"Muthafucka!" I yelled then tossed my phone on the table.

It was the tenth time I called him and the tenth time I got sent to voicemail. It was after midnight and I was more than worried about his ass. It had been over six shootings today and I felt in my gut they all had something to do with that stupid chain and even dumber video.

I was working at the shop when faith sent it to me. I couldn't believe Jamar had really did that shit. That wasn't even his style.

"It's really on now bitch!" She yelled in my ear.

"You think this shit coo? Juice gon' lose his fuckin' mind."

"Fuck'em, he thinks he way too hard anyways. About time some niggaz put him in his place." She shot back.

I kept pacing in the living room hoping Jamar wasn't lying in the street somewhere dead. I kept feeling like the whole beef was all my fault and would never forgive myself if he died. I should have just fully cut Juice off as soon as Jamar came home instead of leading him on. I shook my head at how much of a thot I was acting like. I touched my stomach and really couldn't believe I let myself get knocked up. The whole time I was with Juice I'd never gotten pregnant and now I was carrying his child. Part of me felt like it was destiny, while the other part wanted to get an abortion. I still hadn't decided. I heard Jamar putting his keys in the door. I got happy and mad as fuck at the same time!

I yanked the door open then threw my hand on my hip. "Where the hell you been? What, you ain't see me calling you!" I yelled in his face.

He looked like he'd been up for three days straight and wasn't wearing the clothes he'd left in this morning. Now he had on black from head to toe and I knew exactly what that meant. My eyes got stuck on Juice's chain that hung from his neck like he bought it. He smirked after he saw what I was focused on.

"Stop yelling before you wake my son up." He kissed my forehead then walked in like everything was normal.

"Jamar, why you been ignoring my calls?" I asked real calmly.

He sat down. "I've been busy, I couldn't talk."

"Doing what?"

"You know what."

I shook my head. "You shouldn't have bought that chain and you damn sho' shouldn't have made that video. What are you doing?"

"Why not? He the boogie man or somethin'? I'm posed to fear him?" He was getting mad.

"You don't understand what that chain means to him, Jamar. You don't know how he thinks, but I do. If you have it then nobody is safe. Nobody is innocent. He's gonna start killing anybody that's associated with you. I'm telling you, baby," I tried to reason with him.

"So, what should I do? Go ahead and say it, Naughty." He leaned in closer.

I swallowed hard. "Give it back, baby. You don't gotta squash the beef, but get rid of that chain," I kept it real.

He jumped up. "So, you want me to be a bitch ass nigga? I'm not giving that pussy his chain back. Fuck that nigga! You know what the streets will say about me?" he spat.

"It's better than being dead!" I blurted my real feelings. He took a step back with a look of hurt on his face. His eyes went from sadness to fury within seconds and I knew I'd fucked up. *Shit.*

"There we go, finally I get the truth out of you," He stepped in my face. "This ain't about no innocent people or none of that shit you was saying. This about me huh? You don't think I can win a war against him, huh? You think I'ma bitch?"

I shook my head. "I will never think that about you, I know you."

"Then what is it?"

"You have a heart, he doesn't. You have morals that you live by, he doesn't baby. He killed an innocent pregnant girl just for fuckin' with a nigga. He doesn't care. And now you took from him what he loves the most. He'll kill you, me, and our son over that stupid chain." I broke down crying.

He pulled me into his chest. "He really did a number on you, baby girl. He got you believing he's Freddy Krueger or some shit." He started laughing.

I pulled away. I couldn't believe he was making fun of me like I was a joke. He was becoming way too arrogant for his own good.

"You're a fuckin idiot!" I yelled then stormed off to the room.

I wake up the next morning and Jamar was nowhere to be found. He never came and got in the bed.

Stupid ass nigga. I had an idea that I knew would set him the fuck off, but he'd left me with no choice. I fed my son then dropped him off at my mama's house. The plan that I had would only bring me misery but at least my son would have his father alive. I called my brother.

"I'm on my way to yo house right now and It's very important that Juice is there." I hung up before. I lost my nerve and went home.

I pulled up to JoJo's twenty minutes later, but I sat in the car for ten minutes making sure I was doing the right thing. The more I thought, the more I realized that Jamar was right. I didn't think he could win a war against Juice. I knew he wasn't no bitch, but he wasn't no monster either. Juice was. I exhaled away my nervousness then stepped into the cold early morning September air.

"Must be real serious to have you sitting in the car for so long," JoJo said as soon as I walked in.

He was sitting on the couch going through his phone no doubt texting some thot. I looked at the two guns on the table, shook my head then sat down next to him. I was too close for comfort because he looked at me weird then scooted away a lil'. I grabbed his hand then stared into his eyes.

"I really need your help convincing Juice not to kill Jamar."

He recoiled. "Impossible. That nigga gotta die, sis."

"I'm pregnant by Juice." I blurted out.

It took fifteen minutes for Juice to storm into the house. I had already given lil bro the game plan and he reluctantly agreed to help me with Juice. He claimed I didn't have a chance, but I knew I did. I knew he still loved me more than anything and I could force him to see the light.

"What's good, gang?" He shook JoJo up then sat down across from us.

He looked like he hadn't eaten or slept in at least a week. He looked like he was high out of his mind which wasn't good for anybody, but once he locked his demonic pupils on mine, I knew he wasn't the same Davontae I'd fallen in love with. He was a lost soul, but I felt like I could revive him.

"What the fuck you want, traitor?" He spat.

I played with my thumbs then spoke. "For you to please not kill Jamar."

I saw the fire dance in his eyes before he hopped off the couch. I was glad JoJo was there to protect me.

"You brought me over here to listen to her beg for a dead man's life? I'm starting to think you on some traitor shit too nigga!" He yelled at JoJo.

I saw Juice slightly move his hand towards his waist

"Never that blood. Sis gotta deal that she wanna offer you." He let the insult slide off his back.

"If this deal don't involve you setting that nigga up, then I don't wanna hear it. You got some fuckin' nerve even showing yo face. You probably just got done fuckin that nigga while he had on my brotha's chain!"

"I wouldn't do that Juice." I almost started crying from his spiteful words.

"Ain't no telling what you would do. I don't know you anymore, you're a traitor. You might wanna stay out the public with that sucka cause I'm not hesitating," he promised then walked away.

I couldn't speak. The look he had me made me feel like the scum of the earth. I knew I'd hurt him and there was nothing I could do to fix it. I decided to just let him leave. I looked at JoJo then put my head down. I heard the door open then JoJo told my darkest secret.

"She's pregnant by you, blood."

Juice froze for a few seconds then closed the door. He refused to look at me though. That was the last thing he was expecting to hear.

"How you know it's mine?" He still wouldn't turn around.

"I'd just got off my period and we didn't have sex until after I knew I was pregnant."

He spun around. "So, you fucked another nigga while my child is in your stomach?" Flames shot from his mouth.

"Juice, can you please just stop?" I begged

"Naw fuck that shit!" You ain't about to be with that nigga now! Now I'm really killin' him!" he exploded.

"I'm not gonna be with either of you if you agree to my deal."

"Speak."

"If you promise not to kill Jamar, I'll leave him and have your baby. If it's a boy, I'll even give you custody. And I'll steal your chain back for you," I spoke fast.

"But you're not gonna be with me?" He sounded hurt.

I shook my head. "I'm not gonna be with you or him!" I kept it real.

"He'll never agree to this shit and you know it."

"When I threaten to leave with you and his son, I bet he will."

He ran his hands through his dreads for a few seconds deep in thought, then he stared right through me.

"No deal. I'ma kill that bitch then drag yo ass back to our condo while you're still pregnant. That's the new deal."

"If you kill Jamar, I'ma get an abortion," I threatened.

JoJo hopped up and grabbed Juice in the nick of time because he was about to choke me out. He lunged straight for my throat!

"Fall back nigga! This my sister!" JoJo yelled.

Juice regained his composure then faced me.

"Now, you're dead to me. If you kill my child, then I'ma kill you. After that, me and yo' brotha can kill each other." He stared me up and down then walked out.

He wasn't playing. I saw it all in his eyes.

"That wasn't a part of the fuckin' plan!" JoJo yelled at me.

I put my head in my lap and started crying. It was the only thing I had control of.

Chapter 28
Juice

It took us over a week to catch Lil Teflon lackin' but when I got the call from flash, I cracked my first smile in weeks. The whole squad had been rotating stakeout duties since I'd first got the drop. We knew it was only a matter of time before we caught up with him. I was chilling at me and Brittney's old apartment when I got the call from Flash that Lil Teflon's Charger was parked. *That's yo' ass!* I jumped off the couch and headed to the northeast. Thankfully, I was already pushing my scandalous ass Nissan, so I was able to drive straight there.

The universe worked in mysterious ways of that I was sure. Cause right before the call I was sitting around thinking about Naughty. One half of me still loved her while the other half wanted her dead. I kept picturing her taking dick while my seed was inside of her. Just the thought had me seeing red. I even texted her a few times over the past couple of days, but her position remained the same. I was seriously debating on kidnapping her.

"This nigga dying tonight on my brotha grave," I vowed to Flash.

I shook my nigga up and said soon as I hopped in. I couldn't wait to put his bitch ass in a wooden coffin.

"Yeah, it's a wrap for blood. We gon' do 'em real foul too for all that social media shit they been on." He responded

I looked around to see if anybody was outside that could identify us later on. I didn't see anybody. I checked the time, it was a lil past six o'clock. The sun wasn't down yet but it wasn't outshining either.

"You see his bitch's purple Benz yet?" I asked.

He shook his head "Naw, I ain't seen nobody come or leave, gang. The Charger was already there when I pulled up."

I nodded. We knew his bitch Kim drove the Benz because we'd spotted her leaving and coming multiple times. We could have been crushed her but that would have been pointless and fucked our mission up. We had the drop of the year and needed to make it count to the max. We wanted Lil Teflon dead.

"Aight, we gon' post 'til the sun goes down then we runnin' in there. You tell anybody else?"

"Nah, I hit you first. I knew you wanted the first piece of action at these bitch ass niggaz."

"Good lookin' gang." I shook him up again.

We sat in silence for ten minutes before he spoke again. I was picturing myself standing over Jamar putting a hollow tip in his head when he fucked my visual up.

"You and TJ need to speak, the shit ain't right, gang."

I slapped my forehead. "If he got a problem that's on him. I don't even think about the nigga," I said.

"Juice, you put a gun in his face."

"He tried to stop my mission; he knows better."

"No, he tried to stop you from getting killed by the pigs or going to jail. He did that out of love, and you know it." He shot back.

I shrugged my shoulders. "Maybe so, but he's been challenging me on every issue he can ever since we got the plug. He acts like I'm tryna be a dictator or something. He clearly got a problem following my lead. He might need his own team."

"Y'all trippin!"

"It is what it is my nigga."

TJ was the least of my worries. I'd barely even thought about the triv with him. His options were simple, listen and get rich or fall back and be broke. I turned the nigga from a half not to a half got and his level of appreciation was real low. I didn't have time to be babysitting no grown-ass man. Shit, I barely had time for my daughters.

"There she goes." Flash tapped me on the shoulder.

I came back to reality and saw the purple Benz parking right in front of the house. I slid down in my seat. My mind started racing on how to handle the situation. I lowkey wanted to snatch the bitch up and force her to let us is but I didn't want the neighbors to see us and call the pigs. The last thing we needed was to be inside their spot and the police showed up catching us red-handed.

"We might still gotta wait brody. I don't want no nosey ass neighbors to see us run in the spot," I told him.

"It doesn't matter. We can pull an all-nighter and catch his bitch ass in the morning."

"Naw, we ain't doing all that. We runnin' in that bitch when the sun goes down."

We watched Kim get out grocery bags then headed to the house with the door open.

"It's still bags left," Flash said.

I gripped the Glizzy in my palm tryna keep my emotions in check. But when she walked in the house leaving the door open, I couldn't take it anymore.

"Fuck it, let's just walk right in that bitch and crush 'em."

He didn't respond, he just kept staring at the house. Right when I was about to speak again, Kim walked back out. But this time she was looking behind her while she was talking, and I knew the enemy was right behind her. I could feel it.

"I know his bitch ass bet not show his face or it's on right now, on the gang," Flash vowed.

Lo and behold lil' Teflon walked out like he didn't have a care in the world. He didn't even look around as he followed her to the car. He must have thought niggaz could never bring it to where he rested his head. Most muthafuckaz thought that until their brains got knocked out.

I noticed a bulge on his hip through his sweatpants. I wasn't even kinda worried though, most killaz died with their pistols lying next to them. I know beyond a shadow of a doubt I was dying with mine.

"Let's eat," I growled, then bounced out.

Soon as I got out, he recognized me from across the street. He was just getting ready to reach in the car. He froze for a second no doubt unsure if it was really us showing up at his place of residence. I watched his eyes go from doubt to anger in a split second. But it was too late we up'd on him.

Boom! Boom! Boom! Boom! Boom! Boom!

"Ahh! Ahhh!" Kim screamed out.

Lil Teflon pushed her to the ground then decided to let his nuts hang. He got to bustin' while walking backwards away from his bitch.

Boom! Boom! Boom! Boom! Boom! Boom! Boom!

We were on his ass and he started feeling the heat. He took cover behind a car while still shooting at us. That was the wrong move. We split up and made our way to him taking different sides of the car. He was a sitting duck. By the time he realized he'd fucked up it was too late. He fired a shot then tried to run off like a bitch.

Boom! Boom! Boom!

We lit his back up making him do a retarded ass dance before he dropped his gun then fell to the pavement. The shit was pitiful.

"Roll yo bitch ass over," I kicked him in the side forcing him on his back. "You thought that shit was funny, taking pictures with my brotha's chain huh?" He forced a smile.

"Bitch, fuck yo brotha and that chain! You a bitch ass-"

Boom! Boom! Boom! Boom! Boom!

The bullets to his head and face cut short the tough guy act. If he was really that hard then he wouldn't have tried to run from us. We smirked at each other then left him there for the coroner to scrape up. His bitch was still sitting there screaming her head off. I shook my head at her stupidity. "Should of ran," I told her.

Boom! Boom!

I put one through her face and neck. She jerked back then died with her eyes open staring at the sky. We couldn't leave a witness alive to get us life in a cold-ass cell. *Fuck that!*

***

"I don't know how the fuck that bitch ain't dead. I hit her twice, up close, face shit!" I yelled out in frustration, then punched the dashboard.

"Sometimes that's how the game goes. We know a lot of mutha-fuckaz that's living with a bullet in their head. Y'all just got a bad break, blood, that's all. For now on, we gotta stand on top of shit til the clip empty." Mask replied.

We were sitting outside the strip club 'Dream On' on 162nd and stark the very next night. We knew muthafuckaz wasn't expecting us to strike again so fast, but we were gon' keep applying pressure until those pussies dropped my chain off somewhere.

"I know," I started rubbing my head tryna fight the stress that was building up. "But now we gotta worry about the bitch snitching on us."

"Shit, first she gotta pull through. That bitch on life support and they said it ain't looking good. Worse case, we'll pop her top again. Don't worry about it, we'll take care of it."

That was easy for him to say since he wasn't the one with his life hanging in our enemies' girls' hands. But I'd already vowed to myself that if she lived then I was gon' sneak in her room and smother her with a pillow. Under no circumstance was I going to jail. Fuck That!

"Aye, them Murk Unit niggaz sick huh?" I smirked and stuck my hand out.

"On gang," He shook me up. "But this one gon' let the whole town know how ruthless we are."

We gon' be hot as a muthafucka, but fuck it. We all in now. These niggaz started this shit."

"And we gon' finish it," Mask said, then leaned back, getting comfortable.

I looked at my watch. It was 2 a.m. I knew the last of the strippers and tricks would be coming out any minute. I didn't have the slightest remorse for what we did or were about to do. I'd lost my conscience months ago after we killed anna. She haunted me in my sleep for weeks but now I slept like a baby. Demons couldn't be haunted in their sleep by other demons. I sold my soul to this gangsta shit and the price was cheap.

"There she goes right there." Mask pointed at Tweetie as she walked down the stairs.

"She still bad," I said.

"Fuck that bitch. She shouldn't have fagged off on me back in the day and she would be alive tomorrow. I wish she could see my face, bitch." He slid his mask over his face and spat fire.

I knew my nigga still felt some type of way about how she did him when they were rockin'. I watched him sneak out like a thief in the night with his pistol hanging by his leg. She was walking straight to her car without even thinking of checking her surroundings. She was probably used to niggaz sweating her after the club and just wanted to hurry up and get home. But her home would no longer be on this earth.

Mask must have called her name because she spun around with an attitude then saw the grim reaper himself.

Boc! Boc! Boc!

She dropped to the concrete before she knew what was really happening.

Boc! Boc! Boc!

It was overkill fo'sure. He knocked all her brains out then stared at her for a second. Boc! One more because he was still mad. Mask looked up and saw the bouncer staring at him from the door.

Boc! Boc! Boc!

He sent some hot shit his way until he ran back inside. Mask jogged back to the whip then peeled out the lot.

"Got it out yo system?" I smirked.

"Fuck that bitch nigga."

"They 'bout to be sick as fuck in a few hours. Next time they'll think twice before shooting at us with our kids. The difference is we don't miss."

Chapter 29
Jamar

"Aight, so he ain't dead? Aight, Aight." Flip spoke in his phone then hung up.

"What's crackin'?" I held my arms out.

I was hoping Flip didn't have any more bad news for me. The last few weeks had been real in the town and muthafuckaz wasn't playing by the rules anymore.

"First, them Murda Gang niggaz caught Lil Teflon lackin' and hit his bitch up in the process. Which I could understand, leave no witnesses. But then niggaz did Dirty's big sister real bad. Went up to her job and filled her head with holes just cause Dirty was her brother."

Then of course those Murk Unit niggaz caught Ghost lackin' at the light, but he ain't dead. I think he took a few to his arm and shoulder.

I waved the info off then got off the couch and started pacing. It was me, Flip, and Pusha posted up in my basement tryna figure out our next couple moves.

"I'm not even worried about those drama gang niggaz, they're kids to me. We need to catch Gunna or Juice and knock the soul out 'em. When we strike, we gotta make it count, cuz." I responded.

He nodded his approval. "I'm thinking about making my baby mama stay her ass in the house 'til we're done smoking these niggaz. Cause now niggaz are targeting our bitches, what part of the game is that? It's easy shooting at somebody that can't shoot back."

"Yeah, you right cuz. I might gotta have Naughty fall back on her shop for a while too."

"Good luck with that one," Pusha said, then waved my comment off.

I already knew she was gon' trip about it but it was probably the best move to make. The last thing I wanted to do was explain to my son why his mother was dead and never coming back.

"Nigga we gotta go get something to eat, I'm hungry as fuck!" Flip whined.

"Aight, let me go holla at Naughty real quick then we out," I replied, then made my way to my bedroom.

Naughty was sitting on the bed talking on the phone while my son was playing on his iPad. I loved my family more than anything and knew I had to protect them by any means necessary. It was my job. Naughty looked up at me with an attitude.

"What? Let me guess, you 'bout to go hit the streets with yo niggaz?" She said then rolled her eyes. For some reason, we'd been beefing for the last few weeks and I was reaching my breaking point. I didn't even know why the fuck we weren't feeling each other but I was damn sho' gon' get to the bottom of it.

"Lil Jamar, go to yo room real quick so me and ya mama can talk."

"Okay, dad." He got up and left without taking his eyes from his game.

I walked in then sat on the edge of the bed. I stared a hole through Naughty while she sat there talking on the phone like I wasn't there. I don't know why she kept on trying me like I was a sucka, but she was a few seconds away from getting choked out.

"Bitch I'ma call you back, this nigga 'bout to start trippin." She sucked her teeth then tossed the phone.

The way she looked at me had me ready to snap but I knew she just wanted some attention.

"What now, Jamar?"

"I'm thinking about having you stay away from the shop for a while. You see them bitch ass niggaz are targeting women now and they know how to get to you easily. I know how much yo love to shop but I'ma need you to fall back 'til we done killin' these niggaz off." I gave it to her raw.

"Aww, hell naw!" She snapped her neck like all black women did when they were mad. "I'm not about to sit in the house and let my business suffer cause y'all niggaz wanna shoot at each other. Fuck that!"

I hopped off the bed tired of playing games with her ass. "If I say you are, then you are. You wanna try and challenge me?" I spat.

She crossed her arms and sucked her teeth. "No, I don't wanna challenge you but you're not being fair." She poked her lips out getting ready to start whining.

"And how is that?"

"They're not gonna do anything to me baby and you know it. Think about it. They can't kill JoJo's sister and Juice still loves me. Neither one will allow nothing to happen to me."

I nodded along. I knew what she was saying was the truth, but I wasn't feeling how she was depending on Juice's love for her. She must have noticed the discomfort on my face because she hurried up and compromised.

"You can even have some of your homies sit outside the shop and I'll check in with you every hour on the hour. Pleeaassee!"

I nodded. "I'll think about it and let you know. We 'bout to get something to eat real quick. I'll be back, don't leave," I told her then walked out.

"Thank you, daddy!" she yelled at my back.

***

"We need to find out who's Juice's plug and knock that nigga off. That'll really hit those niggaz where it hurts." Flip suggested.

We were driving down M.L.K Blvd. headed to Taco Bell that sits on the corner of Lombard Street. It was broad day and niggaz were known for getting spanked on MLK. It was the busiest street in Portland and had hella long lights which resulted in multiple murders every year. But we weren't worried about none of that. We gripped out heats at every light and scanned every car hoping we spotted an enemy. Any enemy.

"Shit that ain't gon' ever happen. I heard O-Dawg plugged him in with the head of one of them cartels. How else you think he got on so fuckin' fast?" I replied.

"Yo this line way too fuckin' long," Pusha complained when we turned into the lot.

"Yeah, fuck all that, hit up McDonald's down the street." Flip agreed.

I was just getting ready to pull out the lot when Pusha yelled in my ear.

"Cuz, there go them niggaz right there!" He pointed at the door to the building.

Me and Flip snapped our necks in that direction, and I couldn't believe what I was seeing. Omar and TJ were walking out with smiles on their faces like shit wasn't real. Like they hadn't been shooting innocent women all week.

"We crushin' these niggaz cuz." Flip vowed.

I thought about it for a second then nodded my head. I knew this opportunity wouldn't come around again and we had to capitalize on it. I grabbed the .45 with the fifty-round drum on it off my lap, then bounced out. I was gon' make this shit count. Flip and Pusha were right on the side of me with their poles out ready to kill something. Those pussies must have had their radars on because they both looked at us at the same time and got the surprise of their lives.

Boom! Boom! Boom! Boc! Boc! Boc! Boc! Boc!

Omar's fat ass got his chest filled up with that hot shit soon as he tried to up on us. He got off a shot right before he collapsed to the pavement like a bitch. TJ got to bustin' at us, forcing us to back up a lil while he retreated to his car.

Boom! Boom! Boom! Boom! Blatt! Blatt! Blatt! Blatt!

Everybody around us started screaming and scrambling to get out of death's way. All the cars in the drive-thru started panicking and crashing into each other moving so fast around us TJ was able to escape our line of fire.

"Where the fuck he go?" Flip yelled.

Boom! Boom! Boc! Boc! Boc!

Omar fired from the concrete forcing Flip to spin away from the shots. Pusha and I sent some shots his way, knocking him back on his ass. When the gun fell from his hands as he laid still, I knew he was a goner.

Boom! Boom! Boom!

"Bitch ass nigga!" Flip stood over him confirming the kill this time.

I looked around for any sign of TJ, but his weak ass was long gone. He'd left his mans for dead without the slightest hesitation. *Hoe Nigga!* I hoped to god that when it was my time to go that my niggaz wouldn't fold on me.

"C'mon y'all!" Pusha yelled as he dashed back to the car.

Chapter 30
Naughty

"Bitch, fuck you! You was dead to me, but now I'm going to personally kill you. I can't let you live now. First, you choose that nigga over me, then he gets my brotha's chain, but now he killed Omar! How the fuck can you sleep with the nigga after you claimed to love Omar?" Juice screamed in my ear.

Is he crying? Something told me not to answer the phone for him, but I did anyway. I didn't even know Omar was the one that had gotten killed a few hours earlier. The news hadn't released a name yet. It had been so many recent murders that I'd chopped it up to just another one. But I never expected for it to be Omar. A wave of grief hit me.

"Omar? I never knew he was dead Davontae and how you gon' threaten to kill me when I'm carrying your child?" I whispered.

"Fuck you and that baby bitch! I'ma kill you then cut that muthafucka out yo' stomach and step on it! I didn't want any more kids anyway and especially by no thot ass hoe like you. Keep your eyes open cause I'm comin for you!" he growled and hung up on me.

For the first time in my life, I felt real fear. I felt chills slowly make their way through my whole body. I shuddered from the coldness. I heard the hatred and pain in his voice. He was more than serious. *He's gonna kill me!* Now I understood why Jamar changed his clothes and showered soon as he came home. I knew something was wrong by the look on their faces. *Not Omar.*

My phone went off again as I got out of the bed. I saw it was faith.

"Hello?" I answered as I walked out of the room.

"Bitch they killed Omar!" she yelled in my ear.

"I know, I heard. Juice's crazy ass just called to let me know that he's coming to kill me now." I whispered.

"What? Why? Fuck that nigga anyway, ain't nobody scared of him no more. You need to go get that abortion and wait for his ass to die," she spat.

"I know. Look, I'm 'bout to talk with Jamar. I'll call you when I'm done."

"Don't confess your sins."

"Fuck no," I agreed then hung up.

"Jamar!" I called out as I made my way down to the basement.

"Yeah?"

He was standing by the TV with a gun in his hand. I noticed he had the news on. The look of paranoia on his face told me everything I needed to know. I looked around and realized that his homies were gone.

"What's wrong?" He asked then came over to me.

I busted out crying out of nowhere. I cried because I couldn't tell him about the child inside my stomach. I cried because I had real love for Omar, and I knew many more would die. I cried because I was in fear for my life.

"Why you crying? What happened?" He wrapped me up in his arms.

"Juice just called and said since y'all killed Omar that he's gonna kill me now!" I whined then put my face in his chest.

I felt him tense up. I knew beyond a doubt that he would protect me all the way down to his last breath. Ans with Omar being dead I had a feeling it might come down to that.

"Call yo brotha and tell 'em what that nigga said," he said in my ear.

"Why?" I was confused

"JoJo love you more than anything. If Juice really feels that way, then we can split them up and hurry up and finish the beef. That way you don't have to worry about me and yo brotha ever funking. Divide and conquer.

I thought hard about what he was saying, and it made perfect sense. That way my life could go on with my brother and baby daddy both in it.

"I'ma go call him right now." I pulled my phone out then walked off.

All the love I had for Juice was now dead and gone. I couldn't believe that he really wanted to kill me, and his child just because his friend was dead. He was acting like I was the one that killed him. He had me fucked up!

"JoJo? I need to talk to you right now," I told my brother then broke down crying again.

Chapter 31
Juice

"Fuck you and that baby, bitch! I'ma kill you then cut that mutha-fucka out 'yo stomach and step on it! I didn't want any more kids anyway, and especially by no thot ass hoe like you. Keep 'yo eyes open 'cause I'm coming for you," I growled then hung up on that bitch.

I wiped away the tears that were falling down my face then stuck my face in the plate of powder I had on the kitchen counter. *Sniff! Sniff!* I tilted my head back so I could get the max out of the A1 cocaine I had in my nose. I wiped the tears away again but then they were quickly replaced. I hadn't cried from the soul since I watched my brotha get smoked. I knew one day that the enemy would strike back but damn I wasn't expecting for them to catch Omar lackin'. The shit was hurting me to the core.

"Are you fuckin' serious nigga?!" Brittney yelled from behind me.

I hit the powder again then turned around to face her nagging ass. "Ashley ain't even here, so it don't matter where I get high at. You know Omar just died, so don't come in here naggin me," I growled.

I mugged the shit out of her like she was an opp, but she didn't budge one bit. She had her hand on her hip and was mugging me right back.

"Nigga, I just heard you admit to having that bitch pregnant! And she got you all in your feelings too, talkin' 'bout you gon' kill her and how she chose a nigga over you. You got me fucked up fo'real this time!" she screamed her head off.

Damn, she caught me. It was nothing I could say to defend my-self; I was caught red-handed.

"My nigga just got killed, don't fuck with me right now," I whispered in grief, then turned my back on her to hit the coke again.

Sniff! Sniff! Sniff!

"I don't give a fuck about him being dead! You got that bitch pregnant!"

I froze up instantly. I just knew that I'd heard her wrong. It had to be the drugs playing tricks on me. I turned around to face her.

"What you say?"

"You heard me, nigga! Just cause yo' friend got himself killed, don't mean shit to me! You got that bitch-"

Pow! Pow! Pow!

I hit her ass with a cold combo that sent her flying to the floor. I'd never punched her before but this time I couldn't control myself. She crossed the line at the wrong time.

"Bitch, you done lost yo' fuckin' mind disrespecting me like that," I roared while standing over her.

She held her jaw while staring at me with pure hate.

"I hate you, nigga, and I hope you die in the streets like the rest of yo friends," she spat venom.

All I could do was stare at her and wonder where the fuck did my bitch go? She was far from the innocent woman I'd fallen in love with years ago. Now she was just like the rest of the black nagging ass baby moms in the hood. Maybe it was my fault, but I didn't give a fuck. It was over.

"Keep talking and you'll be dead in minutes bitch."

"Fuck you, I'm done with yo abusive cheating ass," she spoke real calmly.

I nodded. "You can keep the house." I hit the dope one more time then walked out.

I was supposed to go straight to Gunna's house where all the homies were, but I decided to ride around to see if I could catch some opps lackin'. Niggaz loved to celebrate and let their faces be seen after their team dropped somebody. I rode past a few liquor stores and bars but didn't spot any of the enemy's cars. I was hoping to catch anybody that I didn't fuck with or that fucked with the enemies. So, I could take my pain out on them.

I was in my Bentley driving slow as shit so I knew somebody recognized me. The Draco was posted on my lap just begging to be put to work. I parked right across the street from taco bell, where my nigga got smoked at. The detectives still had the parking lot taped up while they did their CSI thing. I shook my head at the sight of my niggaz blood on the pavement. They really did my bro bad, but I was gon' do them even worse.

"Yeah?" I answered my phone.

"Blood we still over here waiting on you," Gunna said, sounding hella impatient.

"I'm almost there." I hung up then pulled off slowly

I shook my head one more time at the crime scene. *Damn Big O.*

Chapter 32
Juice

It was over twenty niggaz packed inside of Gunna's basement. A few of them I had never seen or spoken to before, but I didn't' trip because I knew my niggaz must have trusted them in order for them to be there. I already knew Gunna had a few lil homies under him that he wanted me to meet but I never made the time to. After I was introduced to the niggaz I didn't know they filled me in on a few details I didn't know. The more I listened the more I felt like some shit didn't add up.

"Get TJ on the line," I demanded.

I paced back and forth while Flash called him on speakerphone. It went to voicemail. "Try again." He did and we got the same result.

I looked at each niggaz face in the room to see if they were thinking what I was. Nobody matched my suspicions. Then out of nowhere, I realized that Twin wasn't present with us. That shit didn't sit right either.

"He said he was going to Seattle for a week or so while the heat died down," Flash spoke for him.

"He ain't never left the town before after we dropped somebody, why now?"

"He said they'd just walked out of taco bell when the suckaz got up on 'em. He said they're on camera leaving and he got grazed so his blood is probably on the scene too."

"And?" I stopped pacing so I could face everybody. "He's facing attempted murder at the max and not even that cause the shit would be self-defense. My nigga is laying on a steel slab right now and he thinks it's more important to leave town?"

"So, what you saying?" Mask asked the question the whole room wanted to know.

I stared right into his eyes so he could see how serious I was. "I'm starting to think he backdoored my nigga for the opps. His actions and story ain't adding up to me on the set. That nigga suspect, on me." I spoke what was on my mind.

Everybody looked at me like I was crazy. Like I was the only nigga in the room that was seeing the signs.

"Yo blood," Gunna sat his hand on my shoulder. "You know I'm usually with you, but I can't rock with you on this one. You're talkin' about treason and that means death."

I turned and stared into his eyes. "Nigga, I know what the fuckin' penalty is," I growled. "Why else would he leave the homie to die in the street by himself like a muthafuckin' dog? Huh?! Fuck all that, I'ma go kill his mama and I bet he brings his bitch ass back!" I hurried up and swiped the tears from my eyes. "I would have never left you to die by yourself, fuck that."

He shook me up then gave me a G-hug.

"I know blood, but that doesn't mean that he set bro up just 'cause he got up outta there."

"Bro could have died by the first shot and wasn't nothing TJ could do shit happens," Flash added.

I thought about it, but I wasn't ready to give in yet. "He needs to be here and explain himself. I'm telling y'all right now, If he doesn't show up soon, I'ma kidnap his mom," I spat then looked at JoJo. "What you think?"

He shrugged his shoulders. "I think the big homie is high, paranoid, and looking for somebody to kill."

Maybe I am too high, am I trippin?

I sat my ass down cause my mind was racing way too fast for me. I think I snorted way too many lines and it was starting to catch up with me. I leaned back and tried to gather my thoughts while everybody else started talking. I don't know how long I had zoned out but when my epiphany hit me, I hopped up and cut Gunna off from talking.

"Why that nigga Twin ain't here? Have anybody called 'em? Cause he damn sho' ain't hit me up." My tone was dripping with suspicion.

All my Murda Gang niggaz looked at each other with looks of suspicion now. They knew I was on to something with that one.

"I hit 'em up but he didn't seem to be concerned. He basically said it wasn't his problem." Mask told us.

"Nigga what?! So, all of a sudden he ain't rockin'?" Gunna had flames spitting from his mouth.

Mask shrugged. "Basically."

"He too busy fuckin' with them Inglewood family niggaz," I spat.

The room got quiet for a few seconds as the irony of the situation kicked in.

"One of my niggaz told me that this Inglewood nigga was slanging the same work as we got, but for a lil' cheaper. I thought maybe he copped a large enough supply from y'all so he could be able to do that." JoJo spoke up.

"What's the nigga name?" I asked.

"He from Inglewood. Filmo."

We all shook our heads at each other realizing what was happening. I told Twin not to play with me, but I guess he thought shit was sweet on my end. *Bitch Nigga.*

"Filmo be with Twin all the time," Flash stated the obvious.

"What's the triv? Why I feel like y'all leaving us out the loop about some critical shit?" JoJo leaned forward waiting on an answer.

I never told him about the shit that Twin and Jaxx tried to pull on me. The homies and I felt like that was some in-house shit that his team didn't need to know about. But now that the cat was out of the bag and shit was looking suspect, I had no choice but to give it to him. His life and his homies' lives might depend on it.

"Our plug wanted for me to step to the side for a while and let Twin handle that side of the family," I said through clenched teeth

"What the fuck? Why?!"

I exhaled, then took the next twenty minutes breaking down the triv to the room. After I was done explaining the shit, I had to step outside on the porch to clear my head. That whole situation was taking my anger to a whole other level. I tried to push it out of my head so I could solely focus on the suckaz that took Omar from us.

JoJo came out a few minutes later and sat down next to me. "Here kill this so you can relax a lil," he said then passed me a cup of lean.

My cocaine high had dropped dramatically, and I felt like getting low now anyways. I started sippin' to relax my nerves.

"What's on yo mind nigga?" I asked after noticing him look at me strangely a few times.

"My sista called me cryin' talkin 'bout you was gon' kill her. She told me that you said you were 'bout to come looking for her since Jamar killed Omar. What's up with that? At first, I was kinda trippin' but after hearing you talk about TJ setting Omar up and killin' his mama, I think yo anger has been getting the best of you. You already know you big bruh, but I can't just sit back and let you kill my sista." He spoke his mind while staring into my eyes.

I smiled inside at his bravery. That's why I fucked with the lil' nigga hardbody, he was a brave heart.

"Lil bruh, if I was serious about any of that I would have killed you first 'cause I already know how you give it up. That ain't no disrespect or no shot, just the facts. I did spazz out on her though, gang. I knew the nigga was over there with her and the shit was eating me up knowing that he'd just killed Omar. Feel me? But you know I love her to death and would never hurt that girl. Plus, she carrying my child."

He nodded then shook me up. "I already know, brody."

"Yo, y'all gotta see this shit." Black came outside and said then went back in.

We hopped up and rushed inside. Everybody had their phones out and was staring at 'em with hate. Gunna shoved his in my face. I instantly recognized Glizzy and T-Rex on the screen. They were on Facebook live talking that gangsta shit.

"On my mama cuz, they said cuz had just started biting his taco when he got shot in his face. I know his fat ass eating hella tacos in the afterlife. Fat bitch." Glizzy then took the Backwood from T-Rex.

"They were sitting on the couch in the studio with a few guns laying on the table. They had big ass grins on their faces like they'd just did something worthy. I couldn't stand cheerleader ass niggaz.

"On blood, fuck that nigga. I don't know when these pussies in Portland gon' learn not to fuck with us. Every time one of the suckaz catch us lackin' on camera somebody ends up dying behind it. That acting tough shit for the gram ain't been working for y'all." T-Rex said then started laughing.

I pushed the phone outta my face then started pacing again. I couldn't believe niggaz had the heart to disrespect my manz like that. I didn't know what kinda drugs they were on, but it had just closed their caskets.

"These week ass niggaz are over there talking like ain't nobody gon' die behind my manz or somethin'. Anybody recognize the studio they're in?" I growled.

I wanted to kill somebody the same night to set an example.

JoJo shook his head. "Naw, I don't know where the fuck they're at."

"Somewhere in the cuts," Mask added.

"Fuck!" I screamed out my frustration. "I'm done with this talking shit, on Murda Gang. I'm 'bout to get on a real muthafuckin murder spree!" I walked off and went straight to Gunna's room.

I was tired of sitting around talking, not doing shit. Nobody had a drop on any of the opps so it wasn't shit we could do at the moment and it was killing me. I sat on Gunna's bed and started sipping on the lean while I went over all the problems in my life. I felt a sharp wave of grief hit me as Omar came to mind. I was hurt.

"Juice? Get up nigga!" Gunna shook me

I wiped my eyes and sat up on the bed. I didn't know how long I'd been knocked out. Shit, I didn't even remember going to sleep at all.

"What's good nigga?" I knew something was up by the looks on their faces.

Gunna, JoJo, and Ghost were all staring at me with smirks on their faces.

"One of my square partnas hit me and said he's right in the next room from those suckaz. He saw 'em when they came in and know that I'm fucking with them. He doesn't know if they're still there or not. What you wanna do, blood?" JoJo said.

I hopped up and snatched the Draco off the floor. "We killin' those niggaz, mask up."

"On my dead brotha, I hope these pussies are still in here. I'ma do these lil niggaz bad Gunna, I'm tellin' you right now. Closed casket shit, on the gang!" I growled as we pulled into the studio lot.

I'd been dead silent for the whole fifteen minutes it took to drive over. All I kept thinking about was my nigga laying on a slab while detectives were taking pictures of the coroner removing bullets from his body.

"We gon' crush em tonight or next week, but either way, they're dying," Gunna replied then slid his mask down.

I put on my Obama mask and waited for JoJo to make his move. He and Ghost were parked next to us and I could see him on the phone. Less than a minute later I saw the studio door open up then JoJo and Ghost bounced out. We stepped out into the night then speed-walked into the building. Soon as we hit the hallway JoJo homeboy pointed at a door then disappeared behind his.

Gunna tried the doorknob then nodded at us. It was on. We got in position then I nodded back. Gunna pushed it open, we rushed in like S.W.A.T.

"Murda Gang!" I yelled.

"Drama Gang!"

I saw Glizzy sitting on the couch talking on his phone while T-Rex was in the booth rapping. Glizzy's eyes got wide when he saw us. He knows it was over for him. He went for the gun on the table, but he didn't make it.

Yoppa! Yoppa! Yoppa! Boom! Boom! Boc! Boc!

We knocked his ass back on the couch, he slid down to the floor dead as a Muthafucka.

T-Rex was frozen up like a popsicle behind the microphone. We stared at him the same way a pack of lions did when they have a zebra cornered. We were licking our chops. I saw the other pistol on the table and realized It belonged to him and there was nothing he could do. I picked it up then took my mask off.

"Whoever this is, tell everybody his bitch ass died behind big Omar. If you wanna die next then come get at us, Murda Gang." I hung up then looked over at T-rex.

We locked eyes and I knew he was a real bitch. He was seconds away from crying.

"I got an idea, bring him over here," I said then stared down at Glizzy.

I couldn't believe he was the one that they said killed ace. He was just talking all that tough guy, shoot 'em up shit and now he was laid out with holes all in his face. He looked scared on the ground, nothing like the gangsta he claimed to be.

"C'mon blood, y'all ain't gotta kill me," T-Rex begged as they walked him over.

"I ain't gon' kill you, you're too soft. But if you wanna live you better do what the fuck I tell you. Get on your Facebook live and apologize for what you said, right now." I demanded.

I put my mask back on and stepped back while he logged on. We kept out heats on him just in case he tried some heroic shit.

"Give me that," JoJo growled, then snatched the phone after he was live.

"Speak bitch!" he yelled at him.

T-Rex wiped the sweat from his forehead. "I apologize for speaking on Omar, that wasn't gangsta-"

"You ain't no gangsta," I cut in.

"I shouldn't have done that blood," he continued.

I smiled behind my mask at how much of a bitch he was.

"You see what happens to disrespectful niggaz?" I pointed at Glizzy. JoJo aimed the phone at Glizzy on the floor.

"Yeah, I see him," he replied as he stared at his dead homie.

"Now you can join him, tell Omar It's Murda Gang!"

Yoppa! Yoppa! Yoppa! Boc! Boc! Boom! Boom! Boom! Boom!

His body stood up and took every bullet then collapsed to the floor with smoke coming from it. JoJo got every second of it. He tossed the phone next to their bodies then stood over T-Rex.

Boom! Boom! Boom!

He wanted to get his licks in. We crept out of the room then back to our cars without any hiccups. I still felt sick about my bro being dead, but I did feel a lil better. But I knew until I smoked the niggaz responsible that I wouldn't sleep well at night. What we did was just a lil teaser for the streets. Shit was about to get way worse about Omar being dead. Facts.

Chapter 33
Jamar

"I'm on the way right now cuz, just hold tight," I told Pusha as I put a bag of bricks in the trunk.

"I'm here. Don't trip, she's good. But I still say we go shut that niggaz funeral down, fuck them slobs."

"I told you, If we do that then they gon' come fuck both of ours up in a few days. We can't give them two different opportunities to cook us. Plus, the homies mother and families gon' be in the crossfire, we can't chance that."

"If we kill 'em today then they can't kill us in a few days." He persisted

I hung up in his face while I drove off. I felt where he was coming from, but I knew the shit would backfire on us. Even if we killed one or two of those suckaz, we couldn't catch them all. Then they would come spray up Glizzy and T-Rex funerals fo'sure. They would hit us hard and with a vengeance. I gripped the Uzi with one hand while I steered the wheel with the other. *Fuck That!*

The past week had been nothing but shooting after shooting. They were still tryna purge for Omar and we were out searching for revenge about both the lil' homies. Shit, even Ray-Ray was strapped up now and riding. After that lil' stunt they pulled on Facebook live all types of niggaz were feeling some type of way. A lot of Muthafucka rocked with T-Rex that wasn't from the outset. So, seeing him killed like that sparked even more beef for them. I knew them niggaz were fools, but I didn't think they were that stupid. They were gonna get snitched on fo'sure, it was only a matter of time. After being locked in the house for a few days' Naughty started going crazy, so I gave in and started letting her go to the shop. I always had some of the homies watching the shop just in case the suckaz tried something. But I knew since she was JoJo's sister that it wouldn't happen, but still.

I pulled up to the shop twenty minutes later and parked right next to Pusha. I looked at my watch, 12:10. I knew all the enemies were at the funeral and only about ten minutes away. I wanted to hurry up and get Naughty out of harm's way.

"Good looking my nigga." I shook the homie up through the window.

"You know I got sis, cuz. What you 'bout to do though?" He asked. I noticed he had a gauge laying on his lap.

I shrugged my shoulders. "Take her home and chill for like an hour then pick my son up. After that, we gon' hit the streets and see what's up. What you 'bout to do?"

"Link up wit' Flip and 'nem, I don't know."

"Aight cuz, I'ma fuck wit you later." We shook up again then I made my way to the store.

Chapter 34
Juice

I stared at my nigga in his casket and felt myself go numb. I never in a million years would have thought that he'd get killed before I did. I looked at the all-white suit his mama had him dressed in and shook my head. My nigga hated suits so I couldn't understand for the life of me why he had on one now.

"On my brotha's grave, on your grave, I'ma kill all those bitch ass niggaz so you can crush 'em in the afterlife. Murda Gang forever my nigga." I took the Rolex off my wrist and laid it in the casket. "I'll get it back when I get there, brody. I ain't even gon' lie, it's probably gonna be real soon."

I went back to my seat next to Gunna and watched a bunch of fake muthafuckaz walk up to his casket. Most of the people at the funeral were his family members that he didn't even rock with. I knew for a fact he hadn't spoken to most of them in years. But when one of his fake ass female cousins got to speaking about him on the microphone, I couldn't take it anymore. I was either gon' snatch her ass up by her bad weave or leave the spot. I didn't wanna disrespect his service, so I decided to leave. Once Gunna and the homies saw me walk out they came right behind me. It was me, Gunna, Mask, Flash, and JoJo standing outside in the cold. The drama gang niggaz were still inside paying their respects to the homie but I knew they would be right behind us in the next few minutes. It was only so much fake shit any real nigga could take at once.

"I'm ready to kill one of those fake Muthafuckaz up in there." I vented to the homies. I patted the .40 on my hip out of habit.

"Chill out blood, every funeral in the world got fake shit going on. That's just how it is." Gunna replied.

"Fuck that shit, when I die, I don't want no funeral, on the gang. Just ride for me and I'm hood." Mask said.

"On my mama nigga-" I was cut off.

Boom! Boom! Boom! Boc! Boc! Boc! Boom! Boom!

Gunna shoved me to the ground then started bustin' back. I couldn't believe I was lackin' like that! I knew better than to have my back to the street. I probably would have taken one to the dome if Gunna hadn't saved me. I jumped up and get to blazin' back at the suckaz. Those niggaz were bol

d as a Muthafucka, I'll give 'em that. They came through with no masks on, straight bustin'. I locked in on Flip then aimed straight for the head.

Boc! Boc! Boc! Boom! Boom!

"Fuck Omar!" Dirty yelled, then grabbed his nuts before they all took off down the street.

I gritted my teeth. "Don't run now!" I chased after them tryna cave one of their back in.

They disappeared around the corner like some real bitches, I was hot! I stood there shaking my head while smoke was coming out the barrel. Flip, Dirty, Teflon, and Pusha were dead men walking fo'real.

I jogged back over and saw blood gushing from the top of Mask's chest. I couldn't tell if the bullet had hit his chest or his shoulder area. *Fuck!*

"Keep pressure on it, blood! C'mon!" Gunna yelled at Flash as they were walking him down the stairs towards the car.

"Gas team!" somebody yelled.

Boc! Boc! Boc! Boom! Boom! Boom! Boom!

Those niggaz started shooting from their car that was parked at the corner.

Boc! Boc! Boc!

Me and JoJo started shooting back while we walked up. They let off a few more then skirted off. Now my gangsta really felt disrespected!

"I'm chasing them niggaz! I'll meet y'all later at the hospital!" I took off to my car, then sped down the street hoping to catch them at a light so I could fry their ass.

Chapter 35
Naughty

"Baby, hurry yo ass up, damn." Jamar rushed me for the hundredth time.

"I'm almost done," I said, then hung up the last blouse on the rack.

I looked around and tried to find something else to do but everything was done. I wasn't in no rush to go sit in the house, but my options were limited. Jamar had me on house arrest the last couple of weeks and it was killing me. I'd just recently convinced him to let me come to work but that was bittersweet. Every time I looked up one of his homies was staring at me through the window. They took the shit more seriously than the secret service. But my real issue was getting free so I could get an abortion. Jamar was making it impossible for me to do it though and I knew It was only a matter of time before I started showing.

"I'ma take you and my son out to eat tonight. We gon' hit up one of those five-star restaurants downtown." He told me as we walked through the lot.

I stopped dead in my tracks and looked him right in the eyes. "Are you serious? Don't try to gas me up, Jamar."

"I promise baby." He sealed the deal with a kiss.

I started smiling then speed-walked to the car. I wanted to hurry up and get home so I could get right for my man.

"Oh, now you wanna move fast," he said then started laughing while we hopped in.

I smiled then flipped him off. His phone went off right when he was about to start the car up.

"You can talk and drive." I rushed him.

"I told y'all niggaz not to do that shit cuz!" He roared into the phone.

His anger made me flinch. "Calm down, it's okay." I rubbed his neck.

He sat there listening with the look of the devil on his face. Whatever it was, had him mad as a muthafucka, and I hoped it wouldn't affect our dinner plans. I took my attention off him then noticed a nigga walking towards us with a big ass gun in both his hands and a smirk on his face. I knew for a fact that I recognized him, but I couldn't remember from where. I screamed for my life then pointed at the man coming towards us.

Yoppa! Yoppa! Yoppa! Yoppa! Yoppa! Yoppa!

The windshields were knocked out instantly then Jamar covered me up. I heard him grunt in my ear as he took the bullets for me.

Yoppa! Yoppa! Yoppa! Yoppa! Yoppa! Yoppa!

It felt like he would never stop shooting at us. I prayed that he would then it stopped. I tried to push Jamar off of me, but he was too heavy.

"C'mon baby! Get up, we're okay!" I yelled but he wouldn't move.

The driver door opened, and Jamar was pulled off me. He sat him up like he was about to drive. I stared at the man looking at Jamar like he was surprised or something. Like he didn't recognize him. I looked at my stomach and saw all the blood pouring out. At first, I thought it was Jamar's blood, then suddenly, I was on fire and knew I'd been shot. I gripped my stomach and watched him take Juice's chain off Jamar's neck. That's when I knew who the killer was. I never thought in a million years he would shoot me.

"Please don't kill me, I'm pregnant," I begged. He stepped back and aimed the gun at me.

"You chose the wrong side and I'm not going back to jail. Marry a doctor in the next life," he told me.

All I could think of was the dinner that we would never make. I never heard a sound, everything went black.

Chapter 36
Juice

I'd been speeding for over fifteen minutes tryna hurry up and get to the hospital. I had tears pouring down my face. *No not Naughty!* When Gunna called and served me the news I felt my whole world shatter. He said she still had a pulse when the ambulance got there but it didn't look good. He said somebody hit the car up with a choppa but none of us did it. I was skeptical though because he didn't have any other beef. The goonies were destroyed, and the few left had left town or was hiding like hoes. Naw, I wasn't buying it. Plus, the triv happened less than twenty minutes after the funeral shootout. After I couldn't find those suckaz, I went straight home and got the news soon as I walked in. First, they called and said Mask had only been grazed in the neck. A few minutes later, I get another call saying something different and shit didn't add up.

"Which one of y'all niggaz did it!?" I yelled soon as I parked next to them. I got right up in Mask's face. He had gauze wrapped around his neck and the most motivation to do it.

"None of us blood, we were all together." Gunna stepped in between us.

I stared my nigga in his pitch-black eyes then at Flash's, he nodded.

"Put it on Omar and my big brotha's grave then," I challenged Gunna.

"On Omar and Big Juice, none of us did it, blood." He stared into my eyes.

I felt relieved but confused on who would do it though.

Then I figured one of JoJo's homies must have done it and botched the hit. *Fuck!*

I pulled my phone out and called JoJo. I knew my lil' bro was sick.

"What?" he answered with heat.

"We're outside right now. Y'all in there?"

"Yeah, we coming out. Sis is dead," he said then hung up.

I put my head down. “She died and they’re on their way out right now,” I told them while tryna not to get too choked up.

Nobody said anything, it was nothing to say. The rain started pouring down hard out of nowhere like god himself was crying. I couldn’t believe my bitch was dead and killed over that bitch ass nigga. I shook my head.

“There they go.” Flash pointed them out.

JoJo was walking up fast with about ten lil’ niggaz behind them. All their faces were stone cold. We started walking towards them. I felt my niggaz pain and knew he needed me. He stared me right in the eyes then lifted his gun.

Boom! Boom! Boom! Boca! Boca! Boca! Boca! Boca!

It was on now! We started having a full-fledged shoot-out with our own niggaz. I was glad that I grabbed the Uzi out of the house before I came. I got to waving that muthafucka all around the lot as I made my way behind a car.

“We didn’t kill yo sister, nigga!” I yelled over all the gunshots.

“Stop lying bitch nigga and come get this work!” JoJo yelled back.

He kept walking up like he had a death wish or thought that a bullet couldn’t hurt him. I snuck behind another car and then lined him up. He was focused on the other car while I crept up on the side of him. *Rookie.*

“Drop that shit or I’ma drop you,” I growled with the heat pressed against his head.

“You gon’ have to kill me, blood, cause I ain’t droppin shit,” he vowed, then turned around to face me.

I saw all the pain and anger in his eyes and was feeling the same thing. He was ready to die, I could see it.

“You drop it, nigga,” Black demanded with his gun aimed at me.

Within seconds, everybody was standing in the middle of the lot with their heat aimed at somebody. I had three pointing at me. Gunna had two in his hands each one pointed at a different nigga.

“Black, kill this nigga! I’m ready to die!” JoJo yelled out while still staring me in the eyes.

"But he ain't," Gunna spat, ready to blast Black after he shot me.

We were outnumbered like a muthafucka. But if we had to die, then we were taking a few niggaz down with us.

"I didn't kill Naughty, nigga, and I could have killed you without you knowing it. I don't wanna smoke you, lil' bro," I told JoJo.

"You're a muthafuckin lie and I ain't falling for none of yo mind games either. So, pull the trigga or I'ma up my shit and force everybody's hand."

"Nigga what? Yo Juice, crush that nigga then we'll figure the rest out. I'm ready to play the odds," Mask shot back.

JoJo shrugged. "Yeah, what he said. That part."

The police sirens were getting closer and closer. I knew they would be there in less than a minute. I shook my head.

"Naw, I can't kill my lil bro. He in his feelings right now and ain't thinking straight. He knows I love his sister too much to do her like that. To kill my own unborn child!" I yelled at JoJo.

Just thinking about the child, we would never have had me ready to kill somethin'.

"JoJo, we gotta go, the boys here!" Ghost said.

He took a step closer, forcing my gun deeper into his forehead like it wasn't even there. Our eyes never broke contact.

"I don't believe you, nigga. I know one of y'all did it. The next time we bump heads, somebody gotta die. Period," he vowed then walked off.

His niggaz walked backwards with their guns on us and we did the same thing. We could see the cop lights flying down the street now. We all took off at the same time to the cars.

Chapter 37
Juice

We all went straight to my spot out in Salem. We knew the other spots were compromised and this was the only one that nobody had ever been to. It was the safest place plus Brittney and my daughter were staying at her moms' house. We sat in the living room rollin' multiple backwoods doing our best to calm our nerves. We were glad to escape with our lives and our freedom. And they both were close calls.

"We gon' have to kill the lil' niggaz period. They can't fuck with us so I ain't even worried on blood gang." Gunna vented.

I didn't feel like participating in their conversation. I was too focused tryna figure out who killed Naughty. I knew a silent enemy was the most dangerous enemy.

"It had to be Rico." I blurted out. It was the only thing that made sense to me.

"That pussy fled to Vegas like the rest of the scary-ass niggaz from Portland do," Flash said.

"Don't mean he ain't snuck back in town. It ain't like he ain't a killa, he just got outgunned and had to regroup. He's still dangerous." I replied.

My phone went off and I knew it was O-Dawg by the ringtone. I exhaled my frustration.

"What's good?" I answered.

"Blood, I heard y'all out there falling apart on me. First, Omar gets killed, now yo' bitch dead, and y'all shooting it out with her brother? The streets saying you whacked yo own bitch. Is that true?" he got straight to the point.

"Hell naw, I ain't do it and neither did my niggaz. Somebody else did it-" he cut me off.

"But they died after the funeral got hit up, right?" His tone was skeptical.

"Yeah."

"And what's up with killing niggaz on Facebook? Everybody knows y'all did the shit. That was fuckin' dumb and hot." He lectured.

"It is what it is my nigga. It's a war out here and we gotta pump fear anyway that we can, period."

"You know the bitch Kim just woke up, right?" His question took us by surprise. We all looked at each other and shook our heads in disbelief. We just knew they were gonna pull the plug on her. *FUCK!*

"Naw, I ain't know but I'ma take care of it asap."

"Can't, the pigs are guarding her room day and night. That means she done already made a statement, blood."

"We'll figure something out," I vowed.

We'll see, but until you get yo house in order, I'ma have to fall back on you. Y'all way too hot, my nigga. But I'ma do some real nigga shit and fuck with y'all one last time. I'll give you fifty bricks but you gotta pay for twenty-five of them upfront.

"Bet," I said then hung up.

It was no point in dragging out the conversation when I already knew that his mind was made up. I'd been getting bad news all week, so it wasn't shit to me at the time.

"Now we gotta kill the bitch before she points us out." Flash punched his palm.

"And probably find a new plug too," I said.

"If O-Dawg thinks we gon' sit back and let 'em play us with Twin, then he out of his muthafuckin' mind blood. I'll shoot that pussy right in his head, on me," Gunna spat.

I didn't respond, it was no need to. I was ready for whatever with whoever. Then my phone went off, somebody wanted to Facetime.

"Who dis?" I answered it. But when the screen became clear, I knew exactly who it was.

"The nigga you spent yo whole life looking for you lil slob ass nigga."

Slob? I hadn't been a Blood a day of my life. He was smiling at the screen while holding up my brotha's chain. My brotha that he killed. I'd never felt more hate in my life, literally. Then it all hit me at once. He was the one who killed Naughty and Jamar. But why Jamar? Everybody stared at his bitch ass without saying a word. We were all in shock. He adjusted the camera and over ten niggaz wearing masks came into view.

"I'ma kill you, nigga," I vowed.

He laughed. "Naw, I'ma smoke you just like I did yo weak ass brotha. I'ma get double the hood credit, cuz!"

I hung up on him and threw my phone at the wall, shattering it. "FUCK!" I screamed Just when I thought it couldn't get any worse, it did. I couldn't believe I'd let him get released without my knowing it. I was lackin! Now the whole city wanted me dead, but I was gon' show them wasn't shit sweet over here. My heart had turned cold.

To Be Continued…

The Streets Stained my Soul 3

Coming Soon

Submission Guideline

Submit the first three chapters of your completed manuscript to ldpsubmissions@gmail.com, subject line: Your book's title. The manuscript must be in a .doc file and sent as an attachment. Document should be in Times New Roman, double spaced and in size 12 font. Also, provide your synopsis and full contact information. If sending multiple submissions, they must each be in a separate email.

Have a story but no way to send it electronically? You can still submit to LDP/Ca$h Presents. Send in the first three chapters, written or typed, of your completed manuscript to:

LDP: Submissions Dept
Po Box 944
Stockbridge, Ga 30281

DO NOT send original manuscript. Must be a duplicate.

Provide your synopsis and a cover letter containing your full contact information.

Thanks for considering LDP and Ca$h Presents.

Coming Soon from Lock Down Publications/Ca$h Presents

BOW DOWN TO MY GANGSTA

By **Ca$h**

TORN BETWEEN TWO

By **Coffee**

BLOOD OF A BOSS **VI**

SHADOWS OF THE GAME II

TRAP BASTARD II

By **Askari**

LOYAL TO THE GAME **IV**

By **T.J. & Jelissa**

IF LOVING YOU IS WRONG… **III**

By **Jelissa**

TRUE SAVAGE **VIII**

MIDNIGHT CARTEL IV

DOPE BOY MAGIC IV

CITY OF KINGZ III

By **Chris Green**

BLAST FOR ME **III**

A SAVAGE DOPEBOY III

CUTTHROAT MAFIA III

DUFFLE BAG CARTEL VI

HEARTLESS GOON VI

By **Ghost**

A HUSTLER'S DECEIT III

KILL ZONE **II**

BAE BELONGS TO ME III

A DOPE BOY'S QUEEN III

By **Aryanna**

COKE KINGS V

KING OF THE TRAP III

By **T.J. Edwards**

GORILLAZ IN THE BAY V

3X KRAZY III

De'Kari

THE STREETS ARE CALLING II

Duquie Wilson

KINGPIN KILLAZ IV

STREET KINGS III

PAID IN BLOOD III

CARTEL KILLAZ IV

DOPE GODS III

Hood Rich

SINS OF A HUSTLA II

ASAD

KINGZ OF THE GAME VI

Playa Ray

SLAUGHTER GANG IV

RUTHLESS HEART IV

By Willie Slaughter

FUK SHYT II

By Blakk Diamond

TRAP QUEEN

RICH $AVAGE II

By Troublesome

YAYO V

GHOST MOB II

Stilloan Robinson

CREAM III

By Yolanda Moore

SON OF A DOPE FIEND III

HEAVEN GOT A GHETTO II

By Renta

FOREVER GANGSTA II

GLOCKS ON SATIN SHEETS III

By Adrian Dulan

LOYALTY AIN'T PROMISED III

By Keith Williams

THE PRICE YOU PAY FOR LOVE III

By Destiny Skai

I'M NOTHING WITHOUT HIS LOVE II

SINS OF A THUG II

TO THE THUG I LOVED BEFORE II

By Monet Dragun

LIFE OF A SAVAGE IV

MURDA SEASON IV

GANGLAND CARTEL IV

CHI'RAQ GANGSTAS IV

KILLERS ON ELM STREET IV

JACK BOYZ N DA BRONX II

A DOPEBOY'S DREAM II

By **Romell Tukes**

QUIET MONEY IV

EXTENDED CLIP III

THUG LIFE IV

By **Trai'Quan**

THE STREETS MADE ME III

By **Larry D. Wright**

IF YOU CROSS ME ONCE II

ANGEL III

By **Anthony Fields**

FRIEND OR FOE III

By **Mimi**

SAVAGE STORMS III

By **Meesha**

BLOOD ON THE MONEY III

By J-Blunt

THE STREETS WILL NEVER CLOSE II

By K'ajji

NIGHTMARES OF A HUSTLA III

By King Dream

IN THE ARM OF HIS BOSS

By Jamila

HARD AND RUTHLESS III

MOB TOWN 251 II

By Von Diesel

LEVELS TO THIS SHYT II

By Ah'Million

MOB TIES III

By SayNoMore

BODYMORE MURDERLAND III

By Delmont Player

THE LAST OF THE OGS III

Tranay Adams

FOR THE LOVE OF A BOSS II

By C. D. Blue

Available Now

RESTRAINING ORDER **I & II**

By **CA$H & Coffee**

LOVE KNOWS NO BOUNDARIES **I II & III**

By **Coffee**

RAISED AS A GOON I, II, III & IV

BRED BY THE SLUMS I, II, III

BLAST FOR ME I & II

ROTTEN TO THE CORE I II III

A BRONX TALE I, II, III

DUFFLE BAG CARTEL I II III IV V

HEARTLESS GOON I II III IV V

A SAVAGE DOPEBOY I II

DRUG LORDS I II III

CUTTHROAT MAFIA I II

By **Ghost**

LAY IT DOWN **I & II**

LAST OF A DYING BREED I II

BLOOD STAINS OF A SHOTTA I & II III

By **Jamaica**

LOYAL TO THE GAME I II III

LIFE OF SIN I, II III

By **TJ & Jelissa**

BLOODY COMMAS I & II

SKI MASK CARTEL I II & III

KING OF NEW YORK I II,III IV V

RISE TO POWER I II III

COKE KINGS I II III IV

BORN HEARTLESS I II III IV

KING OF THE TRAP I II

By **T.J. Edwards**

IF LOVING HIM IS WRONG…I & II

LOVE ME EVEN WHEN IT HURTS I II III

By **Jelissa**

WHEN THE STREETS CLAP BACK I & II III

THE HEART OF A SAVAGE I II III

By **Jibril Williams**

A DISTINGUISHED THUG STOLE MY HEART I II & III

LOVE SHOULDN'T HURT I II III IV

RENEGADE BOYS I II III IV

PAID IN KARMA I II III

SAVAGE STORMS I II

By **Meesha**

A GANGSTER'S CODE I &, II III

A GANGSTER'S SYN I II III

THE SAVAGE LIFE I II III

CHAINED TO THE STREETS I II III

BLOOD ON THE MONEY I II

By J-Blunt

PUSH IT TO THE LIMIT

By **Bre' Hayes**

BLOOD OF A BOSS **I, II, III, IV, V**

SHADOWS OF THE GAME

TRAP BASTARD

By **Askari**

THE STREETS BLEED MURDER **I, II & III**

THE HEART OF A GANGSTA I II& III

By **Jerry Jackson**

CUM FOR ME I II III IV V VI VII

An **LDP Erotica Collaboration**

BRIDE OF A HUSTLA **I II & II**

THE FETTI GIRLS **I, II& III**

CORRUPTED BY A GANGSTA I, II III, IV

BLINDED BY HIS LOVE

THE PRICE YOU PAY FOR LOVE I II

DOPE GIRL MAGIC I II III

By **Destiny Skai**

WHEN A GOOD GIRL GOES BAD

By **Adrienne**

THE COST OF LOYALTY I II III

By Kweli

A GANGSTER'S REVENGE **I II III & IV**

THE BOSS MAN'S DAUGHTERS I II III IV V

A SAVAGE LOVE **I & II**

BAE BELONGS TO ME I II

A HUSTLER'S DECEIT I, II, III

WHAT BAD BITCHES DO I, II, III

SOUL OF A MONSTER I II III

KILL ZONE

A DOPE BOY'S QUEEN I II

By **Aryanna**

A KINGPIN'S AMBITON

A KINGPIN'S AMBITION **II**

I MURDER FOR THE DOUGH

By **Ambitious**

TRUE SAVAGE I II III IV V VI VII

DOPE BOY MAGIC I, II, III

MIDNIGHT CARTEL I II III

CITY OF KINGZ I II

By **Chris Green**

A DOPEBOY'S PRAYER

By **Eddie "Wolf" Lee**

THE KING CARTEL **I, II & III**

By **Frank Gresham**

THESE NIGGAS AIN'T LOYAL **I, II & III**

By **Nikki Tee**

GANGSTA SHYT **I II &III**

By **CATO**

THE ULTIMATE BETRAYAL

By **Phoenix**

BOSS'N UP **I , II & III**

By **Royal Nicole**

I LOVE YOU TO DEATH

By Destiny J

I RIDE FOR MY HITTA

I STILL RIDE FOR MY HITTA

By **Misty Holt**

LOVE & CHASIN' PAPER

By **Qay Crockett**

TO DIE IN VAIN

SINS OF A HUSTLA

By **ASAD**

BROOKLYN HUSTLAZ

By **Boogsy Morina**

BROOKLYN ON LOCK I & II

By **Sonovia**

GANGSTA CITY

By **Teddy Duke**

A DRUG KING AND HIS DIAMOND I & II III

A DOPEMAN'S RICHES

HER MAN, MINE'S TOO I, II

CASH MONEY HO'S

THE WIFEY I USED TO BE I II

By Nicole Goosby

TRAPHOUSE KING **I II & III**

KINGPIN KILLAZ I II III

STREET KINGS I II

PAID IN BLOOD **I II**

CARTEL KILLAZ I II III

DOPE GODS I II

By **Hood Rich**

LIPSTICK KILLAH **I, II, III**

CRIME OF PASSION I II & III

FRIEND OR FOE I II

By **Mimi**

STEADY MOBBN' **I, II, III**

THE STREETS STAINED MY SOUL I II

By **Marcellus Allen**

WHO SHOT YA **I, II, III**

SON OF A DOPE FIEND I II

HEAVEN GOT A GHETTO

Renta

GORILLAZ IN THE BAY **I II III IV**

TEARS OF A GANGSTA I II

3X KRAZY I II

DE'KARI

TRIGGADALE I II III

Elijah R. Freeman

GOD BLESS THE TRAPPERS I, II, III

THESE SCANDALOUS STREETS I, II, III

FEAR MY GANGSTA I, II, III IV, V

THESE STREETS DON'T LOVE NOBODY I, II

BURY ME A G I, II, III, IV, V

A GANGSTA'S EMPIRE I, II, III, IV

THE DOPEMAN'S BODYGAURD I II

THE REALEST KILLAZ I II III

THE LAST OF THE OGS I II

Tranay Adams

THE STREETS ARE CALLING

Duquie Wilson

MARRIED TO A BOSS… I II III

By Destiny Skai & Chris Green

KINGZ OF THE GAME I II III IV V

Playa Ray

SLAUGHTER GANG I II III

RUTHLESS HEART I II III

By Willie Slaughter

FUK SHYT

By Blakk Diamond

DON'T F#CK WITH MY HEART I II

By Linnea

ADDICTED TO THE DRAMA I II III

IN THE ARM OF HIS BOSS II

By Jamila

YAYO I II III IV

A SHOOTER'S AMBITION I II

By S. Allen

TRAP GOD I II III

RICH $AVAGE

By Troublesome

FOREVER GANGSTA

GLOCKS ON SATIN SHEETS I II

By Adrian Dulan

TOE TAGZ I II III

LEVELS TO THIS SHYT

By Ah'Million

KINGPIN DREAMS I II III

By Paper Boi Rari

CONFESSIONS OF A GANGSTA I II III

By Nicholas Lock

I'M NOTHING WITHOUT HIS LOVE

SINS OF A THUG

TO THE THUG I LOVED BEFORE

By Monet Dragun

CAUGHT UP IN THE LIFE I II III

By Robert Baptiste

NEW TO THE GAME I II III

MONEY, MURDER & MEMORIES I II III

By **Malik D. Rice**

LIFE OF A SAVAGE I II III

A GANGSTA'S QUR'AN I II III

MURDA SEASON I II III

GANGLAND CARTEL I II III

CHI'RAQ GANGSTAS I II III

KILLERS ON ELM STREET I II III

JACK BOYZ N DA BRONX

A DOPEBOY'S DREAM

By **Romell Tukes**

LOYALTY AIN'T PROMISED I II

By Keith Williams

QUIET MONEY I II III

THUG LIFE I II III

EXTENDED CLIP I II

By **Trai'Quan**

THE STREETS MADE ME I II

By **Larry D. Wright**

THE ULTIMATE SACRIFICE I, II, III, IV, V, VI

KHADIFI

IF YOU CROSS ME ONCE

ANGEL I II

By **Anthony Fields**

THE LIFE OF A HOOD STAR

By Ca$h & Rashia Wilson

THE STREETS WILL NEVER CLOSE

By K'ajji

CREAM I II

By Yolanda Moore

NIGHTMARES OF A HUSTLA I II

By King Dream

CONCRETE KILLA I II

By Kingpen

HARD AND RUTHLESS I II

MOB TOWN 251

By Von Diesel

GHOST MOB II

Stilloan Robinson

MOB TIES I II

By SayNoMore

BODYMORE MURDERLAND I II

By Delmont Player

FOR THE LOVE OF A BOSS

By C. D. Blue

BOOKS BY LDP'S CEO, CA$H

TRUST IN NO MAN

TRUST IN NO MAN 2

TRUST IN NO MAN 3

BONDED BY BLOOD

SHORTY GOT A THUG

THUGS CRY

THUGS CRY 2

THUGS CRY 3

TRUST NO BITCH

TRUST NO BITCH 2

TRUST NO BITCH 3

TIL MY CASKET DROPS

RESTRAINING ORDER

RESTRAINING ORDER 2

IN LOVE WITH A CONVICT

LIFE OF A HOOD STAR